CREEK

SUE BROWN

SHERIFF OF THE CREEK

COLLIER'S CREEK

SUE BROWN

AUTHOR NOTE

Just a note to readers of the whole series…

My book takes place before Elle Keaton's *Mandatory Repairs*.

This is relevant with one of my deputy sheriffs.

BLURB

A grumpy, small-town sheriff loves his dispatcher with the heart of sunshine. And no one is ever going to find out, especially the man he loves. Then danger rolls into town. Will the sheriff step up and protect his love?

Sheriff JD Morgan loves his job as the sheriff of Collier's Creek. It may be a small town, but he loves the place and its people. His roots run deep, and he can't see himself living anywhere else.

He's a little grumpy as he settles into middle-age, but that's okay. He has two passions in life. One secret, one not. Everyone knows about his addiction to coffee, but no one knows he has a secret crush on his young dispatcher, Ben. JD fully intends to keep it that way. He's too old for the kid.

Ben has two ambitions in life. The first is to become a deputy sheriff somewhere far from Collier's Creek, and the second...that one's proving more difficult. He makes it his mission to make his sheriff smile every morning as he hands him coffee. JD is his, make no mistake about it. The sheriff just doesn't know it yet.

Then trouble rolls into town on the back of a Harley and JD discovers Ben has been hiding a secret past. A husband who wants Ben back and won't take no for an answer.

JD is crushed. Ben is terrified.

Will they handle the unexpected husband problem together or will JD leave Ben to face danger alone?

Find out in the small-town romance, the Sheriff of Collier's Creek.

Sheriff of Collier's Creek is the third book in the multi-author series. Each book is stand-alone, but if you enjoy swoon-worthy romance set in a small town, then stay a while. You'll fall in love with the men of Collier's Creek.

JD

*I*ndigo fades to streaks of pinks and purples in the early morning sky as I do my regular circuit of Collier's Creek. I take a deep breath of the fragrant late summer air. It's not fall yet, but I shiver, wishing I'd worn my jacket. My uniform shirt isn't thick enough to protect me from the wind off the mountains.

I walk a little faster down Main Street, hoping to warm up, but as I stop to look in all the windows of the stores, it's probably a waste of time. I love window shopping when there's no one to see me. Chugging coffee from my travel mug, I pause outside Ellis Books and spot a bestseller I've been meaning to buy for weeks. Then I squint at a book on a table in the store. I can just about make out the title. I'm sure that's the thriller I overheard Ben talking about yesterday in the break room. I could visit when the store is open and buy it for him.

Hot dammit. My resolution not to think about Ben is

broken already. It isn't even seven o'clock and yet I can't help my smile at the thought of the sweet guy back in the office. He makes my crusty old heart shatter into a million butterflies at his wide smile, his full lips curving….

I stop abruptly, sloshing hot coffee over my hand as I trip over a box left in the middle of the sidewalk and the lid flies off my mug.

The coffee is hot!

I yelp and shake my hand, sending coffee drops flying everywhere, covering my uniform pants. I scowl at the fresh stains. It has to be the one clean on this morning. I'll be doing laundry late at night, as usual.

I dump the box in the trash. Losing my first cup of coffee of the day doesn't improve my mood. But at least it breaks me from the daydream which haunts every waking hour, sleeping hour, and every shower I have.

Heck no! I'm not going down that route again. I glower at the inch of coffee left in my cup.

"Morning, Sheriff Morgan. Did you spill your coffee again?" Geraldine says cheerfully as she totters by me.

And of course, someone has to see me. It's just my luck it has to be Geraldine. Today she has teal-colored hair and is wearing a kaftan which is supposed to resemble a peacock's tail. Geraldine had told me in great detail when I'd mentioned how bright it was.

"Morning, Miss Geraldine." I force a smile. "Yeah, I'm such a klutz."

Her mutt, Barkasaurus Rex, aka Barky, sniffs at the wet patches on my pants. She tells everyone he's a Bichon Frise but according to those in the know, he's just a mutt. I have no idea. Barky's small and hairy and yappy, and for some reason Geraldine thinks he's possessed. I'm not so sure it's the dog who's possessed.

Barky clearly doesn't find coffee that exciting, because he

continues to drag his owner down the sidewalk to the place he actually wants to visit, the bakery, where there's a treat just for him, as there is every morning.

I stare down at the coffee stains and huff out a breath. I'm being ridiculous. I know that. A forty-two year old man should not be daydreaming about a twenty-one year old with his life ahead of him.

"Will made you a fresh coffee, Sheriff Morgan," Geraldine calls out over her shoulder.

I grimace. Am I really that predictable?

The answer's obvious. Yes, yes I am. I do this every day. I know it, Geraldine knows it, the baristas at the coffee shop know it. Heck, even the damned dog probably knows it.

I stalk toward the coffee shop, CC's, where Will, the sometime barista has another cup of coffee waiting for me, just like always. I don't really understand why a billionaire wants to play at a low-paid job, but he makes really great coffee and his customers love him. I'm sure that's why Cameron, CC's owner, keeps him on.

Will grins at me as I push the door open and he holds out the cup. "Morning, Sheriff."

"You don't need to look so cheerful," I grumble.

Will raises an eyebrow. "You want me to throw it away?"

I growl at him. He laughs at me and hands over the cup. So maybe there's a morning routine and I play right into the townsfolk's hands. I've been doing this for years. I sigh, unable to hold back my pleasure as I take a sip of the strong brew. I should give up making my own coffee. It's nowhere near as good as Will's and Ben's.

Do not think of Ben! Do not think of Ben!

"How are Mav and Colton?" I ask to distract myself. Mav is Will's son and Colton is Will's new boyfriend, the basketball coach. I haven't met Colton yet, but from the chatter he's an asset to Collier's Creek. I make a mental note to talk to him about plans I have for next year's summer camp. Maybe I should introduce myself before I ask him to help.

"They're great." Will's face lights up as he talks about the two most important people in his life.

I listen and smile and try not to be envious of what Will has now. He deserves it after losing his wife.

When Will comes to the end, I ask "Is Cameron around?"

"Not right now. He'll be in later this morning."

"Okay, I'll catch up with him then."

I like to talk to all the store owners on a regular basis. I find out more about what's going on in the town through a casual chat, than I do sitting behind my desk.

"Has there been any more trouble with the bikers?" Will asks as I pay for the coffee.

Last week a motorcycle club visited Collier's Creek and returned the following day. It's not unheard of, but we don't have any reason for them to visit and I don't encourage them to linger.

"Not so far." I furrow my brow. "They don't normally bother us here. I wonder what that's all about."

Will makes a noise of agreement in the back of his throat. "I mentioned it to Ben last night, but I overheard them say they're looking for someone. I meant to tell you yesterday, but I got distracted." The blush heating his cheeks tells me exactly who the distraction was.

"Any idea who?"

I'm going to have a long talk with my favorite dispatcher this morning. This is the kind of information Ben should have told me immediately.

"None. Here's your change. Ben said he'd talk to Deputy Kent."

I hold back another sigh. Of course Ben would talk to Kent and not me. They'd virtually grown up together.

Will smiles at me, glancing over my shoulder.

"Thanks, Will." I turn on my heel, not surprised to see the short woman grinning at me, with a baby strapped to her chest and clutching a little boy in one hand and a bag in the other.

"Morning, Mary Lou."

"Morning, Sheriff," she says cheerfully. "Threw coffee over yourself again?"

I give her a rueful smile. "Don't I always?"

"You always do," she agrees.

I take a deep breath out on the sidewalk, swallowing half the coffee before I do a repeat performance on my uniform, and pull out my phone. I scroll down to the right number.

"Sheriff?" The voice is sleepy and I realize I've probably woken him from a deep sleep.

"Kent, sorry to wake you. Did Ben mention the bikers to you last night?"

I hear rustling, then Kent speaks, sounding more awake. "He called it in. I said I'd talk to you before we did anything. He didn't give me much to go on."

"Okay. I've just spoken to Will and gotten the same impression. Sorry I woke you. We'll talk later."

Kent yawns, mumbles a sleepy "Bye," then he's gone.

"Coming through!"

I hold the door open for Mary Lou, who thanks me and heads off in the opposite direction to me. I take a slow stroll back home, where I've left my car.

I don't need to do a morning patrol of the town, but it's my patch, my home. I've lived here all my life. Even when my mom and dad passed away, I didn't feel the need to move to another town. This is the only place I have a connection to and it holds me here with silken handcuffs.

For some reason the townsfolk likes seeing their grumpy old sheriff throw coffee over himself every morning. If only they knew the reason why. I pull a face. They're never going

SUE BROWN

to know that their sheriff has a crush on the sweet guy who's taken over as the new dispatcher.

My department covers most of the county, but the office is a brick building on the highway at the outskirts of Collier's Creek. I can walk there, but I never know when I have to drive to the other side of my patch. I'm a hands-on sheriff. I hate sitting behind my desk all day and I'll willingly go wherever Ben sends me.

I daydream about him for another five minutes until I reach my house, a large one-story that I'd lived in all my life, inheriting it from my parents. It's nothing special but it's mine and I'm happy there.

Back home, I change my uniform, sighing again. I should buy shares in my favorite laundry detergent. Then I drive the short distance to the office and reverse into my designated parking space. I growl yet again at the woodie wagon encroaching on *my* space.

"Gloria," I bark as I storm into the office. "Move that monstrosity of yours into your space, not mine."

"Yes, Sheriff."

The clerk behind the reception desk stuffs the last of a cannoli in her mouth, grabs her keys, and heads out of the door.

I shake my head. Gloria Lester will never change. She's come home from college and her dad has given her his old car. It had once been his father's. She hates it but if she wants a car, it's this old heap until she saves up to buy her own. I approve of this philosophy. I just wish she learned to park it, or finds another place to park that isn't next to mine.

"Morning, Sheriff."

My heart does this weird flutter just at the sound of his voice. I turn to see Ben Johnson smiling at me from the doorway to the dispatch office and my day is instantly better just seeing the young tousled, blond-haired man.

"Morning, Ben." I scowl because otherwise I'd behave like a teenage boy with his first crush.

Ben holds out my cup. "Coffee or have you worn enough this morning already?"

My glower deepens and Ben's smile morphs into a wicked smirk that still makes my heart flutter.

"Who called you?" I demand.

"Who didn't?" Gloria trills as she comes back in. "They call every morning."

"I'm supposed to maintain a reputation," I growl.

The office goes silent.

I sigh inwardly. "I'm going into my office."

"To sulk," someone whispers. That's Gloria, of course.

"Shhh," someone else hisses. And that's Ben. My heart warms. Ben always has my back.

I've barely parked my butt in my comfortable office chair when someone knocks on my door. I know who it is. "Come in."

Ben walks in with my coffee mug and a plate with two cannolis. "These are made by Gloria's mom for putting up with her daughter."

I stare at him. "She said that?"

Ben's blue-gray eyes twinkle wickedly. "She said that to Aunt Linda who told my momma who told me."

"I am not even going there." I'll eat the cannolis and keep my mouth shut.

Then I remember about the bikers. "Will said he spoke to you about the bikers last night."

Ben frowns, erasing the smile, and my office seems a little darker. I've seriously got to get over my crush.

"Will didn't have much for us to go on. I passed the information to Eric." His frown deepens. "He said we'd need better intel before we could do anything."

Kent has a point. It could be innocuous. On the other

7

hand an MC looking for someone in a town like Collier's Creek could spell trouble.

"I'll look into it," I promise and Ben's smile returns.

"You've gotten sugar on your top lip," he says.

I flush and grumble as I wipe my lip.

"I'll leave you to enjoy them," Ben doesn't bother to hide his mirth as he leaves the office.

I do *not* stare at Ben's tight bubble butt as he sashays out and closes the door. I pick up the cup and sip at the coffee, made perfectly with just the right amount of creamer and sugar. How does Ben get that right too?

As I eat the pastries I hear the noise of the office going about its day and can't help my smile. This is my world. I've been the county sheriff for five years but I've worked here for over a decade. I squint. No, longer than that.

Collier's Creek is where I'm meant to be. I'm even distantly related to the founding father, Jacob Collier. That's not saying much. He's distantly related to a lot of people in the town.

Not to Ben though. I've no connection to Ben. I checked that out when my dreams about him became a little too real.

I sigh and put the half-eaten cannoli on the plate. Ben's too young. I'm old enough to be his father. There are age gaps and then there's ridiculous. There's no way I'll ever tell Ben how I feel about him. I'll keep my passion and desire for him in the depths of my heart. No one will ever find out and I fully intend to keep it that way.

2

COLLIER'S CREEK
small town romance

BEN

"You know you're wasting your time with coffee and cannolis, sunshine," Gloria says. "He's never gonna notice you exist unless you make the first move."

I'd hidden in the break room, leaning against a counter to stare into my cup of coffee, needing a few minutes alone to dream about my favorite law enforcement officer. Of course, Gloria finds me here.

"Short of stripping naked in his office and offering him a lap dance, I don't know what else to do."

Then I turn crimson, because there's inappropriate, and there's crossing the line and setting it alight behind me.

"Gloria, I'm sorry, I—"

Gloria is like the little sister I never wanted. If this got back to my momma...

She giggles and waves her turquoise-tipped hand. "It's not like I didn't know you've got the hots for our dreamy sheriff."

9

I glare at her. "You think he's dreamy?"

Gloria rolls her eyes. "Eww no! He's like…old."

"You don't think he's dreamy?" Now I'm offended on behalf of the sheriff. "You think he's old?"

"Ben, take a breath. Your brain is tied up in knots. Both brains."

I blush again. She's right but she doesn't have to say it out loud. Sheriff JD Morgan ties me up so tight I can barely speak. He's six feet of stocky perfection, all tight muscle. I could look in his smoky blue-gray eyes forever and I want to run my fingers through his dark graying buzzcut. I spend hours imagining running my hands over the hot body under his uniform. One day I want to offer to help take his coffee-covered uniform off.

I jump as Gloria snaps her fingers under my nose.

"I don't need to see that expression on your face." She makes a disgusted sound.

"I don't know what you mean."

"Sure you don't. That's why you're blushing. Look, I know you like the sheriff. Everyone in the office does. Except the man himself. When are you going to tell him?"

"I can't. What if he laughs at me? What if he says no? What if he fires me?"

"Breathe, Ben, breathe!"

I groan and knock my head on the cabinet door. "I'm stupid, aren't I?"

Gloria smirks at me. "Do you need me to answer that?"

I lean my forehead against the cabinet door. "I like him. He's a sweetheart."

"He's always grumpy."

"He's not to me. He likes me."

And he does, I know that. The sheriff treats me with respect. Grumpy respect maybe.

"He's always grumbling at me," Gloria grouses.

I turn to look at her and raise one eyebrow. I practice that in the mirror ever since I saw Sheriff Morgan do it. It's all kinds of hot.

"What?"

"Does it occur to you why he's grumpy with you?"

She wrinkles her brow. "No."

"You come in late everyday. You park in his space everyday. And you treat everyone who comes in here like they're your best friends."

"I know them all," Gloria protests.

"This is a sheriff's office," I point out. "We all know them. You called the criminal they brought in yesterday "Darlin'" and promised you would call his momma."

Gloria squints at me. "That was Sam."

"I know who it is."

"He's your brother."

"I know that too."

I wish I didn't, but yet again my younger brother was found drunk on a bench in the town square. He's only eighteen, not even old enough to drink liquor, but old enough to get into trouble. My momma collects him when he sobers up. The sheriff had looked the other way so far as the deputies hustle him into the drunk tank to dry off, but his patience wouldn't last forever.

"You think I'm doing a bad job?" Gloria asks, distracting me from my thoughts.

"No. You're great at it." She beamed at me and I smile back. It's the truth. Gloria is born to take care of people. She's the best we've ever had at the desk and I speak with a lifetime of experience of living in Collier's Creek. "Just quit parking in the sheriff's space, yeah?"

She grimaces. "I don't mean to. But I can't park that thing, Ben. Mom says I have to dock it. I don't know what that means."

"*Star Trek?* The Enterprise?" I suggest.

Gloria stares blankly at me. I sigh. No one understands when I nerd out about Captain Picard. I used to watch all the series with my dad. An accidental discovery that the sheriff was into Star Trek just like me confirmed we were meant to be together.

"How about I take you out to practice, yeah?"

"I don't know what all the fuss is about," she grumbles.

I open my mouth and she giggles and pretends to take a picture.

"Your face. I won't upset your man."

"He's not my man."

Gloria places a finger over my lips. "Lying is a sin. You know what Pastor Williams says."

I have a lot to say about Pastor Williams, but none of it I want to get back to my momma, so I mime zipping my mouth.

She's right about one thing. Sheriff JD Morgan is my man. He just doesn't know it yet.

* * *

I MEET the sheriff in the parking lot at the end of shift. He looks as surprised to see me as I am to see him.

"Hi, Sheriff Morgan," I sing out. I'm always cheerful when I see him. "Finished for the day?"

He glowers, his usual expression. "I wish. No, just needing fresh air. I'm looking at the budget and all the numbers are running into each other." He looks surprised as if he didn't mean to give me all that information.

"I'm going to my momma's for dinner. She wants to talk to me about my brother," I say, holding back a grimace. "That's gonna be fun."

"Do you want me to talk to her about Sam?"

I blink at the unexpected offer. "Now?"

"Well, I meant another time, but I can do now if you want."

I give him an apologetic smile. "Sorry, I wasn't thinking. Another time would be great. Thanks."

Sheriff Morgan nods. "No problem."

"I'd better go find my momma before she sends out a search party."

"Moms tend to do that," he agrees.

"Did your mom do that?"

"All the time." His smile is wistful, like he's remembering something special.

I know the sheriff's parents died in a car crash just outside the town. He was first on the scene. I wonder how you ever get over anything like that.

"You could come with me," I say impulsively.

"What?" He looks trapped like a deer in headlights.

"Come back to Momma's house. Have a home-cooked meal. I might even avoid the Sam-discussion."

His expression clears. What did he think I was offering him? I mean I would in a heartbeat, but he'd probably sack me for that offer.

"Thanks, but I've got to work tonight." He did seem genuinely sorry though.

"Another time," I suggest and he nods and walks away.

I watch him leave like I always do. I'm disappointed but not surprised. The sheriff always works late. And why would he want to go to dinner with his dispatcher's family, especially when the guy he arrests all the time will be there too. For an instant I resent Sam, then feel guilty, because he's my little brother and I love him, even if he is a pain.

I huff and slide into my car. Errant brothers first, lust of my life second. Even if I wish it was the other way around.

13

* * *

THE EVENING IS JUST as stressful as I expect. Sam is living up to his asshole brother reputation and I can't hold back yelling at him. Momma yells at me and Sam smirks, smug at having won that confrontation. In the end I leave before I'd finished my potroast because I'm just making it worse for Momma, and I don't want to say something I can't walk back.

"I'll call you tomorrow," I promise as I kiss her on the cheek.

Sam throws me a triumphant look as I leave. When did my sweet baby bro turn into such a pain? We used to be friends.

I need a drink—non-alcoholic—before I go home. I aim for Jake's Tap but it's busy and I can't face that many people. Instead I head for Randy's Beer and Wings. It's just as busy but I spy a free booth. Before I get to it, Randy waves me over.

"Hey, kid, are you working tonight?"

I try not to bristle at the 'kid'. He's known me since I was in diapers.

"Not tonight, Randy. What's the problem?"

'Sheriff's forgotten his order again."

"I'll take it over."

Did that sound too enthusiastic?

He looks relieved. "Thanks. I'm three short and I've got a new crowd in tonight."

I look around and see leather jackets over chairs at the back. "You got the bikers in?"

Randy nods. "But they're not causing any trouble."

"Do you want me to help?" I'd worked there in high school and never minded helping out.

"No, but thanks for the offer. Just get the order to the sheriff."

He bustles around and adds wings and mac and cheese and a can of soda to the order. "That's for you, kid. No charge."

"Thanks, Randy."

I take the two bags. As I leave, I feel like I'm being watched. I look over and the bikers are all focused on me. They don't look away when they catch me staring at them. An uneasy shiver runs up my spine. I hope it's a coincidence they're in town.

Eric Kent looks up from his phone calls when I push the door into the office. A few men are dotted around. The office is manned all the time, but it looks as if some are out on patrol. That figures. The sheriff prefers the deputies to be out rather than sitting on their butts. His words, not mine.

"What are you doing here?" he mouths.

I hold up the bags and point to the sheriff's office.

Kent nods and disconnects the call. "Moonlighting as a delivery boy now? Or is it just because it's for the sheriff."

I scowl at him. I refuse to go bright red although by his snicker I fail. "Randy is short-staffed. He asked me to bring it over."

"Go on then, delivery boy." He shoos me away.

I growl under my breath as I knock on the sheriff's door. Eric can be a total ass at times. I'm so annoyed I forget I was going to mention the bikers to him.

There's a pause before the sheriff answers.

'Come in."

The sheriff sounds distracted and he doesn't look up as I walk in with the two bags of takeout. I notice how tired he looks, dark smudges under his eyes. He's worked at least a fifteen hour day so far. It isn't unusual. He works too hard in my opinion.

"Sheriff."

His head shoots up and he stares at me, his mouth open. "Ben, what are you doing back here?"

I hold up the bags. "Randy asked me to deliver your order. He's short-staffed."

The sheriff rolls his eyes. "I told him I'd walk over and pick up my order."

"He said, and I quote, 'The sheriff says he'll pick it up, then he gets distracted and he remembers three hours later.'"

I grin at the way he goes pink.

"I don't do that."

"You always do," I say cheerfully. "But here it is."

"I thought you were at your mom's."

"Have you seen the time?" I say pointedly.

He looks at his watch. I follow his gaze and drool quietly at the short dark hairs curling around the black watch face.

"It's gone nine." He scrubs his eyes. "I can't even remember when I ordered the food."

I snicker. "It was two hours ago. This is fresh."

"I owe them."

"Take a break for thirty minutes. Come have coffee and eat. Randy packed me food too."

"I should get this finished." He stares blankly at his desk as if he's not quite sure what he's doing.

I point to the door. "Go freshen up. I'll make coffee and plate the food."

He grimaces. "I think I've drunk enough coffee today. If I drink any more I'll be buzzing."

"Iced tea?" I suggest.

"That sounds great." He smiles at me gratefully. "The food smells good."

I ignore the knowing looks from Kent and the other deputies as I walk through the office to the break room. I have a sheriff to feed.

The sheriff arrives as I pour the iced tea into a glass and

gazes at the table, laid out with the food. He was right, it does smell amazing.

"I don't know if I'm even hungry now," he mutters.

"Sit down and watch me eat then," I suggest.

He takes a seat and narrows his eyes at me. "Haven't you already eaten? I know your mom. She always feeds you."

"She did. But I can always eat," I say cheerfully, not saying I left halfway through dinner.

Sheriff Morgan shoots me a knowing look. "Tough night?"

"Something like that," I agree. I pick up a wing. "I need comfort food. You should eat."

He does to my amusement, scarfing a plate of wings before he speaks again.

"I'll talk to your mom soon. Sam's going to get into serious trouble if he doesn't stop drinking. I can't ignore it forever."

"I don't know why he even drinks. He hates the taste of liquor."

Neither of us like alcohol that much which Momma said took after our dad. I drink the occasional beer but more to be sociable.

"He seems to have gotten the taste for it now," the sheriff said dryly.

"Sheriff—"

"Call me JD. It's out of office hours."

I beam at him for the offer. "JD."

"Before you ask, I've got the same name as some actor. You probably don't know him."

I wasn't going to ask. I already knew that. Sheriff Jeffrey Dean Morgan. I can see why he calls himself JD. They even look similar. He huffs and keeps eating. I keep my mouth shut.

"You were gonna say something?" I prompt.

"I was?" He thinks for a moment. "Oh yeah, I want to put in sports programs for kids, to focus their energies on something other than getting into trouble."

"It sounds like a good idea, but Sam has left school."

"He didn't go to college?"

"He didn't get the grades."

It had been a source of tension between us. I'd gone to college and dropped out, whereas he'd flunked at school and never had the chance. Anything else we suggested wasn't good enough for him.

"Let me think about it," JD says.

I never thought I'd end my day eating dinner with my sheriff. It's nice even if I am discussing my kid brother. Would it happen again?

3

JD

There's a knock at my office door, then it opens. I look up from yet another report, surprised. Most times people wait for my call so this has to be urgent.

JoBeth, my assistant, pokes her head around the door. "Hey, Sheriff. Good, you're still here."

It's late in the evening, but yeah, I'm here, like always. I like working late when most people have gone home. It's quiet and gives me a chance to finish the reports. No one told me when I became sheriff there would be endless reports to fill in. I lie. The old sheriff did tell me. I just didn't believe him.

My stomach rumbles and I think about the impromptu dinner with Ben. I kinda want that to happen again but... I focus my attention on JoBeth.

"I thought you went home." I check my watch. "Like four hours ago."

She's wearing a pale lemon shirt and jeans, so she'd obviously gotten home at some point, as she'd been wearing a cream blouse and grey pants when she left.

"I did," she says. "But Danny got a call. They're kicking off at Gilligan's."

That's nothing unusual. Gilligan's is a gay bar out of town. It's rougher than the bars in Collier's Creek, but the beer is cheap and the music okay, if you like dressing in leather. I don't go there, for obvious reasons. If I head to a gay bar for a hook-up, I drive to another county where I'm not known.

But for Daniel Hobart, the mayor, to get a call before me, it has to be bad.

I'm reaching for my hat as I say "Why didn't it come through dispatch?"

She presses her lips together. "His brother was there. I was driving past and Danny called and asked me to talk to you."

I stare at her and she shrugs. "It's not something we talk about."

By we, she means her husband. But now I understand why the roundabout communication. Daniel Hobart wouldn't want that news to get out. Don't get me wrong. The mayor is a good guy, but he's traditional, and if the town found out his brother was frequenting Gilligan's it could harm Daniel's election prospects. I have no idea why his brother couldn't have called me. Am I that unapproachable? That's a question for another day.

"Okay, I'm on my way."

"Thanks, Sheriff."

I roll my eyes. "It's out of hours and you still can't call me JD?"

She smirks at me. "Do you ever call my husband 'Danny'?"

"Touché," I growl at her and she laughs as we both vacate the office.

JoBeth heads out before she's spotted, knowing someone will be there, asking her how to do something. I tell her all the time that she would make a great sheriff, a steady hand at the tiller. JoBeth just laughs in my face.

Ray Murphy is the first deputy I see and I wave him over.

"Murphy, round up everyone, we need to get to Gilligan's."

He furrows his brow. "Has this come through dispatch?"

"No, anonymous source. They called me instead. Who's on dispatch?"

I knew it wouldn't be Ben as he did the early shift.

"Tom."

"Okay, I'll tell him. You call everyone to meet us at Gilligan's."

"You're coming too?"

"Yeah."

I don't explain further, but the owner of Gilligan's is a discreet friend of mine. I don't want to see the place closed down through some drunken hooligans acting out.

Murphy nods. "Okay."

I like the fact he doesn't argue. "I'll talk to Tom and follow you there," I say over my shoulder. "Oh, and Murphy?"

"Yeah?"

"Don't take Roberts."

Murphy rolls his eyes. "Like I'm that stupid? And he's on vacation for the next two days. Visiting with his mom."

"Of course. I'd forgotten."

That's a relief. Skip Roberts is one of the few openly homophobic cops we have in the department. He's approaching retirement and I'm not going to fire a man for outdated beliefs as long as he keeps them to himself, and I mean keeps his mouth zippered tightly shut. He and I had a long conversation about that when I took over as sheriff. I thought he understood, then I heard one too many nasty jokes aimed Ben's way when he joined us. Not in Ben's hearing but loud enough that the other deputies heard. Ben is liked in the office. He's smart and picks the right deputies for the calls that come in. My guys appreciate that. I gave Roberts the option of early retirement or a closed mouth. He picked the latter as he had to pay off his mortgage and take care of his elderly momma. Roberts needs the job and he leaves Ben alone. I'll be glad when he retires though.

I jog down the hallway to dispatch. My heart races just at the thought and I tell it to calm down because Ben isn't there. It doesn't listen.

Tom raises his head as I walk in. He's a family man who likes working nights as his wife works days and it suits with the kids. "Everything okay, Sheriff?"

"Yeah, we're going out to Gilligan's. I got a call to say it's getting a bit lively there." I raise a hand as he frowns. "Yeah, it was a call to me. But we're going out there now."

"'Kay."

"I don't think we'll be long."

"Roberts?

"On vacation."

I see the look of relief on Tom's face too. They're old fishing buddies but Tom knows his friend's limitations.

We pile onto the highway toward Gilligan's. I take the rear. I know some sheriffs always liked to lead. Sheriff Bob from the next county is one of them. But I prefer to be the last resort. Deployed when necessary. I know some of my deputies call me that. Sheriff Last Resort. Yeah, I don't like it, but whatever.

As soon as we reach Gilligan's, it's obvious why it's lively. Twenty motorcycles line up outside the bar.

We walk into the bar. I take stock of what's going around us. It's loud, but whereas I expected a brawl, everyone's minding their own business, dancing, drinking, making out. Two bikers press ice packs to their cheeks, the others standing around them, clearly guarding their backs.

Murphy glances at me, confusion written all over him. "So where's the fight?"

I shrug. "I guess it's over. I'll go talk to the bartenders."

"I'll talk to the bikers," Murphy says.

I sweep the barroom first, nodding my head at the bartenders who just look resigned at our presence. It's not like we haven't been here before. Most of the guys I know by sight, if not by reputation. The bikers are talking furiously with Murphy and Warren. I'm staying back. They can deploy me if necessary. Then I spot two guys in the corner and I narrow my eyes.

What the heck are you doing here?

Ben is squeezed in the corner, trying not to attract anyone's attention, least of all mine. He's partially hidden by a guy wearing a leather harness and leather trousers which was why I didn't spot him before. Ben catches my gaze and I can feel his mortification at his boss and his department gatecrashing his night out. At least he's not in leather. I'm not sure if I could cope with leather and bare skin.

I resist the urge to stalk over and demand to know what the hell he's doing in Gilligan's.

It ain't rocket science, Morgan.

He's young, free, and single, despite the yearnings of his middle-aged boss.

I catch Warren's eye and ask him to talk to the bartenders. He flirts with the young guys and I see them melt in response. Maybe I need lessons.

Then I glance at Ben and catch his gaze. I nod toward the back. Ben stands and his companion tries to hold onto him,

23

but he evades him and slips out of the back door. I resist the urge to tell the kid to keep his hands off my man.

Murphy's got everything under control so I disappear out the door and around the building to meet Ben.

"What are you all doing here?" Ben looks furious under the dim lighting.

"I got a call there was trouble." I fix him with a look. "What are *you* doing at Gilligan's? It doesn't seem your kinda thing."

Ben huffs. "It's not. A friend called me. Craig. He wanted someone to go with him and I was the only one stupid enough to say yes."

Relief eased the knot inside me that had taken up residence since I saw Ben sitting in the corner. I have got to get over my desire to mark him as mine.

"Your friend is the one in leather?"

Ben is wearing a tight T-shirt and even tighter jeans. How he got into the jeans I have no idea, but the denim clings like a second skin.

"Yeah. He's a good guy but into stronger stuff than I am. I just wanted to make sure he didn't get himself into any trouble."

"That's kind of you." I regard him for a long moment and he squirms a little. He's not happy at being discovered here. I'll reassure him no one gives a crap, but after I get the information I need.

"Gonna tell me what happened tonight?"

Ben wrinkles his nose. "Two of the bikers kicked off, brawling with each other. But it was over in minutes. They were pulled apart and told to sit down and behave by the other guys in their club. I don't even know why someone called you."

I'm confused too. No one calls the cops for a couple of black eyes.

"Did they know they were in a gay club?"

He shrugs. "No idea but they didn't seem to care about the guys dancing and making out. They were calm until the fight."

It doesn't make sense but I'll talk to Murphy later and see if he's gotten any sense out of the bikers.

"It was fine until you guys gatecrashed the party," Ben snaps suddenly.

I regard him in silence for a moment and he flushes.

"I'm sorry, Sheriff. I'm bored out of my skull because these guys are not my type. I'm desperate to go home because I've got an early shift tomorrow, but I promised Craig I'd take care of him."

I want to ask what is his type. But instead I nod. "Tell your friend the night is over and you need to be out before the boys kick off again. Sheriff's orders. If he gives you any trouble, call me."

Every member of staff has my cell number and they know they can call me at any time.

Ben gives me a wan smile. "Thanks, Sheriff."

I don't say he can call me JD. This is official business.

"Do you want me to wait until you both leave?"

He gives me a sideways look. "You really think there'll be trouble?"

"I don't know," I say honestly. "I don't know these guys. Bikers tend to stay out of Collier's Creek."

We have our bikers' towns in the county but Collier's Creek isn't one of them. I don't know why they're here and that's what bothers me. I like to have information. These guys didn't want to spill.

"Benny, what are you doing out here? Oh hello!"

Ben's friend lurched toward us, clearly drunk. He's two seconds from face-planting the asphalt. I glance at Ben who looks resigned.

"I'm driving Craig home. I know what he's like."

I nod, knowing Ben understood my expression. I don't tolerate drunk driving on my roads.

"Are you a cop?"

Craig looks up at me, a wide-eyed flirty expression as if I'm some kind of god, but Ben hauls him back before he can touch me.

"Sheriff Morgan," I say. "And you are?"

"Craig," he says breathlessly. "Benny, this is your sheriff."

Even under the dim light I can see Ben is crimson.

"But he's the one you're always talking about."

"Shut up, Craig," Ben snaps.

I cough, amused, and Ben flushes deeper.

"Take Craig home. I'll see you in the morning," I suggest.

"I don't want to go home," Craig whines. "It's too early."

"It's plenty late enough for you," Ben says, shoving him toward a Ford parked in the far corner of the lot. It's not Ben's usual ride.

I watch them get into the truck and drive out of the parking lot. Ben waves at me as they go. I breathe easier once they're away from Gilligan's. Tomorrow I'm going to have a long conversation with my dispatcher about staying away from this bar. My sweet guy is so out of his depth.

Two bikes leave at the same time, their engines rumbling loudly in the night as they go in the same direction as the truck. I frown, wondering where they're going.

"Sheriff Morgan?"

Murphy jogs over to me. "Is Ben gone?"

"Yes." I side-eye him. "You saw him?"

"I saw the way he was trying to hide in the corner." Murphy snorts. "I won't say anything. It's none of my business. I'm just glad he's out of here."

"He's driving his friend home."

"The twink in leather?"

I nod, holding back a laugh at my church-going deputy throwing 'twink' around. Ben's influenced us all.

"Good. Ben needs to tell his friend he'll be eaten alive in this bar."

"I think that's why he was here. To keep the kid out of trouble."

"That boy is too nice for his own good," Murphy says.

"I hear you. So what's happening with the bar?"

"It's closing for the night. The bikers are being encouraged to go home. They're okay. The ones that can drive are taking the others home."

"Are they the guys driving through Collier's Creek?" I ask.

"Yeah. Their leader's got a relative here or something. None of them seemed too sure. Anyway, they're nice enough."

"What was the fight about?"

Murphy shrugs. "None of them seem to know or care. Tell your 'anonymous source' to wait five seconds before calling us out next time."

I sigh and knuckle my eyes. "I need sleep more than I need to know what these bohos are up to."

"Go home," Murphy orders. "It's all quiet. We ain't arresting anyone. You can give me your statement tomorrow."

"I'll see you in the morning."

Murphy rolls his eyes but nods. "See you tomorrow."

I head over to my car. It could have been a lot worse. I'd had nights at Gilligan's where we'd arrested half the clientele. No one arrested and Ben home safely. I count that as a win.

I send a quick text to the mayor telling him all is calm and receive a thumbs up in response. Idly, I wonder if his brother will ever be able to step out of the mayor's closet. Maybe

27

going to Gilligan's is a start, but it's a rough place and the mayor won't be pleased.

That's a conversation I'll have with him another time. For now, I just want to drive home without totaling my car and fall into bed to dream of a sweet, blond-haired dispatcher. I bet he'll be dressed in leather in my dreams.

4

COLLIER'S CREEK
small town romance

BEN

I spend the days after Gilligan's hiding from the Sheriff. I leave him his coffee and cannolis in his office but can't face him after that night. To be caught in a gay bar is one thing, but to be caught in Gilligan's by the sheriff and most of the department is another matter. I'm not sure why I'm so embarrassed. They all know I'm gay. The only one who's going to be furious if she finds out is my momma. She made me promise when I came out to her to stay away from that place.

But no one says anything to me and the sheriff doesn't come near me.

Today starts out rough because soon after I start my shift, I take a call for a serious accident on the highway out of town. No fatalities, thank goodness, but a little girl spends her seventh birthday in the hospital with life-changing injuries.

It creates a pall over the office. No one likes to deal with serious accidents and the deputies return subdued.

"How is Maggie?" I ask Eric when we meet in the break room.

He pulls a face. "Not good. They're not sure they can save her right leg."

I send up a silent prayer for Maggie and her parents. I know them through Momma's church. She's a good kid, feisty, and always on the go. She reminds me of Gloria.

I'll give Momma a call later and see if there's anything she can do for the family, although I have no doubt the Collier's Creek information chain will already be on high alert.

"I hear you were hooking up the other night," Eric sneered.

My blood runs cold. Have the deputies been talking about me behind my back, all of them laughing at me?

"I didn't know you liked leather, Johnson."

"Kent, that's enough."

I turn to see the sheriff standing in the doorway, glowering at Eric. My mouth goes dry and I lick my lips. My heart patters so fast I'm surprised the two men can't hear it. I swallow hard, trying to get myself under control.

"It was only a joke," Eric sneers. "Johnson can take a joke."

"No one gets laughed at for their lifestyle," Sheriff Morgan says sternly.

I want to groan and knock my head against the cabinet. It makes me sound like I'm a wannabe twink for a leather daddy. I know the sheriff means well but he really needs to stop trying to defend me. It will only make it worse with Eric.

Eric curls his lip, but he nods at me and stalks out of the break room leaving me wishing I was anywhere but here.

The sheriff fixes me with a look that's stern and gentle at

the same time. "I don't know how he found out about you at Gilligan's but it wasn't from me."

I nod because one thing I know about JD Morgan is that he isn't a gossip. "Any of them could have told him, even by accident."

'The only person who saw you was Murphy and he's not going to tell anyone."

I shrug helplessly. "It's a small town, Sheriff. And Eric likes winding me up. Anyway, it doesn't matter. It's small potatoes compared to little Maggie."

He nods. "Maggie deserves our focus, but you know I won't let anyone demean you."

I hold back a smile. He's like a grizzly mother hen, flapping over his brood of chicks, and I love him for it.

"I'm gonna call my momma. See if the coven can take care of Maggie and her family."

He raises one eyebrow and I blush.

"Don't tell her I said that."

"You call the church ladies a coven?"

"Only when she can't hear me."

"What's it worth to keep quiet?" He waggles his eyebrows.

Did my sheriff just make a joke? Gloria will never believe me.

"Cannolis for the week?"

"You buy me those anyway," he points out solemnly.

"I'm going to have to up my game."

Our gazes lock and it would have gotten kind of ridiculous but Gloria bursts into the break room.

"Sheriff, have you seen Ben? Oh, there you are. Helena wants to go on her break." She seems oblivious to the tension between us.

He stands back to let me pass. "Remember what I said."

I'm not sure if he means Eric or not, but I nod and smile anyway.

31

As for my co-worker, she'd noticed the way I was hiding from the sheriff earlier and wheedled it out of me as we headed for dispatch. I swear that girl could work for the CIA. There are no such things as secrets around Gloria Lester.

"Kent is a total piece of work," she snarls.

"He's just trying to yank my chain. I should just laugh it off."

"You tell me if he does it again."

In the normal world, I should be the one protecting Gloria. But if the sheriff is the mother hen, Gloria is the warrior. Me? I'm the one providing the coffee and pastries. Oh lord, that makes me the cook.

Helena scowls at me when I walk in. "Did you get lost between here and the break room?"

"Sorry, I was talking to Sheriff Morgan about helping Maggie's family."

Immediately, her scowl eases and she says, "Can your mom help her?"

"I'll call her on my break."

Helena vanishes which leaves Gloria staring at me. I don't trust the look in her eyes.

"What?"

"Line-dancing."

Of all the things to come out of her mouth, line dancing isn't what I expect.

"What about it?"

"Let's go line dancing tonight."

I squint at Gloria. "You've got to be joking."

"Oh come on, it'll be fun," she wheedles. "Randy is hosting a night with the 4 C's."

"You want me to go line dancing."

She nods.

"In Randy's Grill & Wings."

"Yup."

"With the Collier's Creek Cowboy Combo."

Gloria gives me the side-eye. "You know I just said this to you, right? You don't have to repeat it back. It's not a TV show."

"Gloria, I don't line dance."

"How do you know? You've never done it."

"That's not true."

"Old Mrs. Stephenson's class doesn't count. None of us had a clue what steps she was trying to teach us."

This is true. She's been teaching line dancing at the high school since God invented time. I swear the woman is about ninety, although Gloria assures me she's nearer seventy.

"I don't want to go line dancing," I say.

I don't want to go out at all. Ever. In case the Sheriff catches me.

Gloria rolls her eyes because she knows why I'm prevaricating. "It was one time and there was nothing wrong with you being there. You're over twenty-one."

"The cops raided the bar."

"They came because there was a report of trouble."

"And I was there."

Gloria huffs. "You can't hide forever, Johnson. It's not like there's going to be a raid on line dancing night. When was the last time anything went down in Randy's?"

This is true. No one wants to get barred from the place that does the best beer and wings in town.

"It's one night and I need a friend," Gloria says.

"That's what Craig said."

Her lips twitch. "I promise not to dress up in leather."

I groan and she snickers.

"It's not like Sheriff Morgan will be seen dead line dancing."

"He eats at Randy's all the time," I say without thinking and her eyes light up like the tree at Christmastime.

"Uh-huh. Well, sugar, I'm not going to ask how you know that nugget of information, but I have it on good authority—"

"Your mom."

Because there's only one person Gloria listens to.

"Of course. She told me the sheriff is going up to Twisted Pine Ranch tonight, so you can dance away and your man won't see you make an idiot of yourself."

"Thanks, Gloria." I give her the side-eye but she ignores me. "You can go off people, you know?"

"But not me. You love me."

"Don't push it," I growl, but she just laughs, gives me a hug and runs back to her desk before she gets into trouble with the sheriff for deserting her post.

"I'm not going line dancing," I say out loud, but I know it's a lost cause. What Gloria wants, Gloria gets, and it does sound fun, particularly as I know I won't bump into JD. I'm kind of sick of hiding in my house. I just haven't told her how bad I am at dancing.

* * *

THE COLLIER'S CREEK COWBOY COMBO is more enthusiastic than talented, but they're still better than I am at dancing. I trip over my feet yet again and fall on my ass.

Gloria stares down at me in amazement. "How can you be this bad?"

"Do you have to yell it to the room?" I hiss as she hauls me off the floor. The girl is strong.

"I don't have to yell it, Ben. The whole room can see."

"She's right there," Burl says as he sashays past me. "How many times have you fallen over? Four? Five?"

I scowl at him. "Three times and I just can't dance."

I can do many other things but I was born with two left

feet. I grumble under my breath. Did I mention JD is there, watching me make an ass of myself?

'I thought the sheriff was supposed to be going to the ranch?" I hiss in Gloria's ear.

"Burl wanted a night off from cooking so he drove down and they decided to come here. The sheriff can't cook."

I don't ask how she knows that. Her mom knows every-thing. Burl is the cook at Twisted Pine Ranch. I know him vaguely. Momma knows him better.

But that means the sheriff watched me make an idiot of myself all evening.

"I knew this was a bad idea," I grumble.

Five minutes later I'm back on the floor. This time it's the sheriff who hauls me up.

Ground, swallow me whole, please.

The ground ignores my plea.

"Are you hurt?" he asks, looking concerned.

"My butt and my pride. You always seem to rescue me."

"That's my job," he teases.

I brush my ass. It's going to hurt tomorrow, I can tell. I growl at Gloria who just laughs at me and shuffles away. I can't help wondering if she knew this was going to happen.

"Come on," JD says. "I'll show you want to do."

"I think it's a lost cause," I admit. "I don't know how to dance. I just shuffle from side to side."

"Nonsense," he says briskly. "It's just practice. Look, if Geraldine can do it, you can."

"That's a low blow."

"It's a challenge. You gonna step up?"

If it were anyone else, I would have cried uncle and limped back to the booth to drown my sorrows in a fresh soda. But JD is looking at me expectantly and I sigh. "Okay, JD. Show me what to do."

I stand at the end of the line, JD next to me. This is going to be a total disaster, I know it. He's a bigger klutz than I am.

"Just follow me," he says. "I'll tell you what to do."

It'll be over soon, I tell myself and prepare to hold the sheriff up while he's the one falling over.

At the end of the second dance I gape at him. "How did you learn to dance so well?"

Neither of us has fallen over and more to the point, JD is clearly good at line dancing. Better than good. His feet don't go in ten different directions like mine do. But I haven't hit the floor once.

I watch him and listen to his instructions. His voice rumbles in my ear and I have to tell myself to focus. But I stay upright. I could do this all night.

He looks sheepish. "My mom and dad loved line dancing and dragged me along rather than get a babysitter. I hated them for it, but I was good at it and it was fun."

"You must have gotten destroyed at school."

"I told my parents that if anyone found out I would never go dancing again."

"So no one found out?"

He gives a rueful chuckle. "What do you think? Other parents from my school were there. They told their kids who couldn't wait to tell everyone at school. It was a nightmare."

My poor sheriff. I'd been the butt of the jocks' humor too many times. "What did you do?"

"Mom gave me the option to stay at home, but I liked dancing and it was something we could do together." He shrugs. "I stopped when Mom and Dad…"

I cringe at the sadness that crosses his face, knowing what he's thinking. "I'm sorry, Sheriff."

He pats my shoulder. "It's okay, Ben. It was a long time ago. I like thinking about them."

And I like the open way he shows his love for his family. I just wish I could show my love for him as freely.

"Come on," JD says. "They're just starting a new dance."

"Shoot me now," I mutter.

"What?" He glances at me.

"I said, lead me to it."

"You're doing well, Ben. I'm proud of you," he says and he looks genuinely proud.

I can't help preening under the praise. "I couldn't have done it without you."

"It's easy to line dance," he says.

I look around at the other dancers laughing and enjoying themselves and sigh. "Easy for you, maybe. Your feet go in the right direction."

He chuckles. "You just need practice."

"Do you want to sit down?" I ask hopefully.

"One more dance. Come on," JD says. "It's easier than it looks."

"Sure it is."

"Ben," he says, exasperated, but with a hint of amusement in his voice. "Just follow my lead. You'll be fine."

I take a deep breath and nod. We squeeze back onto the dance floor. I never realized how popular this night was with the locals. The band launches into the next number, and he starts moving. I try to follow him. This is more complicated than the previous dances, but JD squeezes my hand reassuringly and gives me simple instructions. I'm just getting the hang of it when the song ends, and we stop moving, to my utter relief. I look up at JD, and he's smiling at me.

"You did great," he says.

"Thanks to you."

We smile at each other, kind of awkward, but nice, and stay like that for a few moments, lost in our own world.

Then the spell is broken by someone tapping JD on the shoulder.

He turns around, and I see a look of resignation cross his face. It's Missy Hawthorne, and she's wearing a tight-fitting red dress that leaves little to the imagination and matching red cowboy boots. She's pretty enough and I know plenty of guys who would love to date her. I'm one hundred per cent sure JD isn't one of them.

"Hey, Sheriff," she purrs. "Wanna dance?"

I can feel the jealousy boiling inside me, but I try to keep it in check. JD is clearly uncomfortable, and I don't want to make it worse.

"Sorry, ma'am," he says. "I'm here with someone."

My heart sinks. He's here with someone? Who? Where are they? Why has he been dancing with me? Then he glances at me and the corner of his mouth twitches. He means me! I really am that kid on a first date.

Missy pouts. "Oh, come on. Just one dance."

"Not tonight, Missy," I say. "The sheriff is helping me learn to line dance. I'm hopeless." I give her a conspiratorial grin, hoping she'll get the message.

She looks disappointed, then winks at me and sashays away. I'm not sure what message Missy received but I see her making a beeline for Burl.

JD lets out a long breath. "You have no idea how grateful I am. Missy is...persistent."

I smirk at him. "Show me how to dance before she comes back."

JD nudges me back into the line. We move together, our bodies in sync with the crowd. Well, he's in sync. I'm working on it. But I don't care what anyone else in the line is doing. It feels like we're in a world of two, and nothing else matters.

5

COLLIER'S CREEK

JD

lie awake most of the night, reliving my evening with Ben. It was the least romantic dancing ever. We'd been in a crowd of people, yet it could have been just the two of us. He wasn't in my arms, we weren't even touching, except when I occasionally nudged him to go in the other direction, but it felt like we were dancing together.

At the end of the night, we'd said goodnight and gone in opposite directions. He'd walked Gloria home and I'd spent an hour chewing the fat with Burl and promising I'd drive up to Twisted Pine soon so he could cook me a proper meal.

By the time I get up, my eyes are gritty and I have the beginning of a headache from lack of sleep. I don't even bother making a coffee and just head to CC's. At some point I'm going to have to break my CC's coffee habit. Today is not that day.

The girl behind the counter takes one look at me and hands over a takeout cup without a word. I must look bad. As

I walk out of the shop, the coffee goes flying and a demon dog ends up with a coffee shower as he jumps up at me and catches me where no man wants to be shoved.

I'm not sure who shrieks the loudest; me, Geraldine, or Barky.

I gasp in pain and hang onto the nearest chair as Geraldine scolds me and croons over her dog. I want to point out he was the one to slam into my balls, but I'm too busy wheezing.

Despite the agonizing pain, I keep it together and apologize for scaring Barky. I buy us all a drink to calm down and to give me time for the pain to subside. Geraldine is clearly upset but Barky has to be okay by the way he inhales his drink, sitting on *my* tender lap, and everyone at CC's kinda laughs but nicely.

I walk them home and we continue our talk about growing up in Collier's Creek. At her gate, Geraldine gives me a wide smile.

"Thank you, Sheriff. No one takes the time to talk with me and Barky anymore except the nice people in CC's."

What do I say? I mumble something about it being my pleasure and we'll have to do it again. Then I head home to change my coffee and fur-covered pants.

I'm late getting into the office and yet again the woodie wagon is parked half in my space. I abandon my car and I stalk into the office.

"Gloria," I bellow.

She looked up, grabs her keys, and rushes by me. "Sorry, Sheriff Morgan. I forgot."

I don't even have to explain why I'm annoyed. "I'm gonna have to teach her how to park," I mutter as I walk toward my office.

"Not you," Ben says as he passes me. "Get one of the deputies to do it. You'll just scare her."

I stop and turn to glare at his retreating back. Me? *Scare Gloria*? It's more likely to be the other way around. Ben carries on, oblivious to my scowl.

Gloria returns, mutters another apology, and now it's my turn to park my car. Gloria's vehicle is parked at an angle but at least I can get in my space. I reverse my car in, cut the engine, and knock my head gently against the steering wheel. It's been a heck of a day and it's not even nine o'clock.

There's no sign of Ben as I head toward my office. Where's my shy smile and the cup and pastries? It's not until I don't have it that I miss his morning greeting.

"Morning, Sheriff." Aimee greets me with a smirk. "I heard about your breakfast with Geraldine and Barkasaurus."

I glower at her. "I suppose it's all around town."

"Yup," she agrees cheerfully. "No one can believe you cuddled Barky."

Nor can I to be honest. What was I thinking? Once Barky settled down and had his treat he was almost sweet, and only tried to nip me once.

I shut the door behind me and knock my head against the wood with a sigh. It's going to be a long, long day. I can just tell.

Then I look at my desk. On one side is a steaming cup, *my cup*, and a plate of pastries. I can't help my smile. He didn't forget. He never forgets. I should know better.

I eat my third breakfast of the day as I read my emails. Jake's Day is coming up. I need to remember to finish my speech. In fairness, I give the same speech every year, just adding in what had happened over the previous year.

After a couple of hours I need a break and I venture out of my office. I turn the corner to find Ted Warren pressing Ben against the wall.

"We could make it a night out," he's saying, almost

purring in Ben's ear. "You and me, away from this office and Collier's Creek. What do you think?"

I'm a half second from throwing our resident flirt out of my office and telling him not to come back.

Ted Warren is handsome and muscled. Think Tom of Finland, in a deputy's uniform. Muscles on muscles. I've seen girls drool when he smiles at them, and men who I'd swear were straight forget what they were talking about as he walks up to them. One even walked into a streetlight he was so busy staring at Tom...I mean, Ted.

He's also much closer to Ben's age. They'd look great together. A perfect couple.

"No thanks, Ted. I'm kinda busy for the foreseeable future." Ben slips out from underneath his muscled biceps. "But thanks for the offer."

He spots me watching the two of them, his cheeks flushing crimson. "Sheriff Morgan."

Ted turns and catches my scowl. "Sheriff."

"Am I going to have to repeat the discussion we had last week and the week before, Warren?" He and I have these discussions on repeat. If it wasn't for the fact he was a damn fine officer, he'd have been out on his ear long ago.

"No, sir. It was just a friendly chat, wasn't it, Ben?"

Ben nods. It isn't like he can say anything else. He knows Ted's reputation the same as we all do. Still, I'm coming to the end of my patience.

"Ben, whatever you were doing. Warren, come with me."

Ben hurries off and Warren follows me sheepishly into my office. I point to a seat and then I sit down behind my desk and glare at him. "You're playing with fire, Deputy Warren."

Particularly when you think you can hassle my *man.*

* * *

I NEED A DRINK. It's been a long day. I stride into the break room and stop abruptly. Just by the coffeemaker I discover Gloria with her hands all over Ben's shoulders and back.

Seriously? Again!

I open my mouth ready to explode at her when Ben groans. I stop, biting back my angry words. That sounds like Ben is enjoying whatever she's doing. That groan makes my toes curl. I want to be the one touching Ben, making him emit noises like that.

I'm about to back away when Gloria looks up, but she doesn't take her hands off Ben.

"Hi, Sheriff Morgan."

Ben stiffens and he whips around to see me in the doorway. "Oh, no."

I raise an eyebrow. "Oh no?"

Gloria giggles. "I know this looks bad, but we've finished our shifts and Ben twisted his shoulder earlier. I was just trying to get the knots out. I'm trained."

"You're a trained masseuse?"

"No, but I've watched You Tube videos."

I have no idea what to say to that.

Ben groans again, not in pleasure this time. "As bad as that sounds, Gloria's got magic hands. She really should take classes. My shoulders feel so much better." He rolls his shoulders. "I mean it, Glor. This feels great."

Gloria steps away from him and I can breathe again.

"Mom always says I should."

"Why don't you?" I ask.

I don't know much about Gloria but it seems more of a fit than a reception clerk.

She shrugs. "I can do that as a hobby. I wanted to work here. I want to be a dispatcher like Ben."

"She's good," Ben assures me. "Gloria takes over on my breaks and people like her."

I look at Gloria with new respect. "Maybe we can talk about this another time. I need someone reliable to cover dispatch, especially as Josie is leaving to have her baby soon."

Gloria's face lights up and so does Ben's.

"Thanks. Sheriff."

She takes a step forward as if she's about to hug me. I brace for impact. But Ben hauls her back and she stops in her tracks to my relief.

"Oh, yeah, sorry, Sheriff Morgan. I forget. But that would be great. Mom'll be stoked."

I know Gloria's mother. She'll be gobsmacked. I want the best for all my staff and that means not putting them in jobs where they're not suited. But I trust Ben not to set Gloria up to fail.

She vanishes with a wave of her hand, leaving Ben and I staring at each other.

It's just getting awkward and I still want coffee but Ben's between me and the coffee maker.

"Sometimes I feel I just want to hide," he says suddenly. "People are always in my space."

I clench my jaw and hold back the words on the tip of my tongue because I don't want to sound like a jealous lover. And I'd been in his space last night.

Ben huffs and runs a hand through his hair. "There's only one person I want to get close to me."

My heart sinks. I'm too late. There's someone else and I've missed my chance. Then I realize he's looking at me. I mean, *really* looking at me.

"I know somewhere you could relax for a while before you go home," I blurt out and wait for him to turn me down politely.

"Great." His smile lights up the break room.

"Give me fifteen minutes and I'll be ready to go."

"I'm off shift. I'll make drinks for us both. Uh...Sheriff?"

"Yeah?"

"Why don't I meet you somewhere? You know what they're like here. If we leave together, the whole town will know. It'll be Barky Mark II."

I had to force myself not to ask if he wants to sit on my lap. "That's a good idea." I say, my voice sounding strangled.

He gives me an odd look. "Where shall we meet?"

"By the large rock."

The large rock was just that. A huge rock at the edge of the town limits on the highway. Tourists park there if they want to go cycling for the day. This time of day the informal parking lot would be empty.

"I'll see you there."

I grunt and vanish out of the break room. I really hope he makes good on his promise to bring coffee with him.

But thirty minutes later, I pull up just beyond the large rock to find Ben in the lights of my car. He's tucked his vehicle out of sight of the highway and I do the same thing. We don't need anyone stopping to be nosy.

Ben leans against the hood of his car, drinking from a takeout cup.

I wind down the window. "I hope you've got one of those for me."

"Have I ever let you down?" He holds out a second cup. "I can't promise how hot it is now."

I turn off the engine and get out of the vehicle. He hands me the cup. I take a long swallow of the cooling liquid and sigh happily. "You went to CC's." Even cool, it's still great coffee.

"I promised Momma I'd pick up bear claws for her."

"You've got to leave now?" I can't help the wave of disappointment that floods me. I'd hoped to have a few minutes alone with Ben.

He shakes his head. "Not yet. I told her I needed to

45

decompress before I came over. She's good about that kind of thing. She gives me space."

"You've got a good relationship with her."

"Mainly," he says cheerfully but he doesn't add to it. "Where are we going, Sheriff?"

"Call me JD now we're out of the office, and we're going to my favorite place when I want to decompress," I say, reaching in to get out a blanket. I'm aware of his curious gaze on the blanket. "I like watching the stars, but I'm too old to sit on the hard rock."

"Very sensible," he says and doesn't even bother to hide his amusement.

I growl and he outright laughs.

"Where are we going?" he asks when he sobers.

"We can walk from here. It's just a glade where we can watch the stars."

"Lead on."

I do as he says, the moon and starlight guiding the way. There's no chance of falling into a ravine here. It's just a small glade in the middle of a patch of pines I've come to think as mine.

I worry all the way if I've just made a huge mistake. If I was Ben's age, maybe I'd suggest we go clubbing and he can work out his frustration that way. But I'm a middle-aged guy who's taken him to look at the stars. Maybe he'll think I'm weird. I go cold at the thought.

But as soon as we reach the glade, I spread out the blanket and Ben flops down onto it with a relieved sigh. As Ben lays down on the blanket, I notice the way his shirt clings to his chest, showing off his lean physique. Averting my gaze, I feel guilty for even having such thoughts. But then he turns to me with a smile, and I can't help but feel a flutter in my stomach.

"It's been a long day," he says.

I settle down at the very edge of the blanket. I don't want

him to think I'm in his space. "Lie back and look up at the stars. You'll feel better, I promise."

"You're right, this is nice," he says after a few minutes, his voice soft and soothing.

I can feel the tension between us growing. It's like the air is charged with electricity and one spark will set it off. I wonder if it's just me and my hopeless dreams.

Suddenly, he turns to me, his eyes locking with mine. "Do you ever feel like you're meant for something bigger than this?" he asks, his voice barely above a whisper.

6

BEN

*I*gnoring the hard stones which seemed determined to make a piñata of my back, I lie on the blanket. Every atom in my body is aware of the man laying next to me. I don't know whether I want to put more distance between us or beg him to take me into his arms. At least the darkness hides how aroused I am.

He's your boss, you idiot.

No matter how much I think of the moldy vegetables in my refrigerator or Grandpa sneezing out his teeth into his tea, my dick doesn't subside. It doesn't care who JD is. It just wants to get up close and personal with my sheriff.

Think! Think, Ben! What to talk about?

If there's one time I need Gloria here. Maybe I need a Gloria sitting on my shoulder. I shudder at that idea.

"Do you ever feel like you're meant for something bigger than this?" I blurt out.

JD sighs and looks up at the stars. "Not really. I'm content in my corner of the world and I like my job."

I roll over on my side to face him. "You don't want to live anywhere else?"

"I don't think I do. I love my town and my county. I made peace with the fact I'm a small-town cop a long time ago." He looks at me. "What about you? You moved away for college. Did you find your dreams?"

Tears prickle the back of my eyes and I'm glad for the darkness. He doesn't need to find out how my dreams of big city life were crushed beneath a biker boot. "Not that time," I say lightly, relieved when he doesn't pursue the conversation.

A cold breeze makes me shiver.

"Are you cold?" he asks. "You can take my jacket."

"No," I lie. "Anyway, you'd be cold then."

It's not only the cold that sends goosebumps over me in a wave, but his proximity. I can feel his warmth even though he's not touching me.

"Aren't they beautiful?"

"Uh…yeah." I'm confused by the question until I realize he's staring up at the sky again.

But then I look up at the stars and I understand what he's seeing, as they blaze across the night sky. I don't often see the stars as bright as this, away from the light pollution in town.

"Each star is so clear," I marvel. I want to reach up and pluck them from the night sky. "Do you know the constellations?"

"I haven't got a clue," he confesses sheepishly. "I keep meaning to learn, but I just spend my time staring up at them."

I chuckle. "That makes me feel a lot better."

JD makes a noise I take to be agreement in the back of his throat. "I come here a lot when I want to think."

I turn my head to look at him. Starlight dances across his

strong features. I want to run my fingers over him. Instead I talk, before I do something stupid, like kiss him.

"Do you ever regret running for sheriff?"

There's a long pause which I don't expect. I always thought JD lived for being a cop.

"Sometimes. I always knew I was born to be a cop but becoming sheriff is a different game. The buck stops with me."

"You don't like that authority?"

"I worry about getting it wrong," he confesses.

"That never happens."

His chuckle is low and rueful. "That's nice of you but it's not true. I screw up all the time."

I gaze up at the stars for a moment, trying to think of one time he got something that wrong. Maybe it's because I'm shut away in the dispatcher's office, but I don't see it. I know there's times he's changed his mind about how to handle a situation but generally he's level-headed and calm. That's why I like him.

"I think some folk wish I was more alpha male."

I chuckle. "You mean like Sheriff Bob?"

"You notice that too?" He teases me and it makes me go warm inside.

"We can't all be Navy SEALS."

"Ouch. I'm definitely not a Navy SEAL. I'm just a small-town sheriff."

I roll over onto my side to face him. "You're the right person for Collier's Creek."

"I think so too," he agreed. "We're a great little town."

"I was talking about you."

He laughs but it sounds self-conscious. My sheriff is shy under that dour exterior. "You're sweet to say so."

"I'm serious."

"Thanks," he says. "You know I appreciate what you do

for the county. You have to take care of them when they need help."

"I know. It's what a dispatcher does." It's my turn to feel self-conscious.

"But we need more people like you."

"Yeah? Like me?" I ask. I turn to face him and he's so close. A kiss would be so easy. I'd barely need to lean forward.

"You have a sense of responsibility. You care about people."

"I do."

"You're a good person, Ben."

I'm so close to him now but I'm not sure if he's going to kiss me or not.

I would let him, I know that much. All the adrenaline pumping through me is desperate for it.

He leans in closer to me, his breath hot against my cheek. I close my eyes and wait for his lips to meet mine. But just as I think hallelujah, it's going to happen, he pulls back.

"I can't," he murmurs, his voice low and husky.

"Can't what?" I ask, even though I already know the answer.

"Kiss you. I can't do this."

"What do you mean?" I sit up, feeling cold and exposed without his warmth beside me.

"I mean, I can't be with you like this. I'm your boss, Ben. It's not appropriate."

"Kiss me. Just once. Please." I beg because I'm never going to get this opportunity again.

I'm in love with him and I'm sure he's in love with me. We're both lonely and we have this connection that's crazy and I know he feels that too. Maybe I'm projecting, but I just want a kiss.

"Just once." He rumbles the words almost against my lips.

I feel his breath warm against my skin and I'm ready to close the gap when he pulls away again.

"I can't do this to you," he says. "You deserve a good guy."

"You're a good person," I protest because it's true.

He doesn't say anything for a moment and I worry that I'm going to cry again. But he only says, "I'm not the right man for you, Ben."

I swallow hard, not wanting JD to see how frustrated I am. "Is this because of the department?"

"No," he says, "not entirely."

"I don't understand. You want me. I know you do."

"I do," he admits. "I want you so much it's made me crazy. But I can't do this to you."

"JD, I'm not a kid. I'm not going to lose my job if I'm with you. This is ridiculous."

"You won't lose your job, but I will."

I press my lips together, frustrated. All I'm asking for is one kiss under the stars. But I know he's right. It's not just about our jobs. It's about our whole lives in this small town. If we start this, it could get messy. What if we can't keep it a secret? What if things go wrong? We can't afford to take that risk.

"I'm sorry," he whispers, and I can hear the pain in his voice.

"It's okay," I say, even though it's not. I'm hurt and confused, but I don't blame him. He's doing the right thing. We both are.

The night is chilly and silent, almost too quiet, as we lie on the blanket, gazing up at the stars. Now each star seems so far away and unattainable, just like my relationship with JD. He's next to me, yet it feels as if he's a million miles away.

We stay like that for what seems like hours before JD sits up and glances down at me.

"We should go. You're shivering."

I want to protest, begging to stay in that peaceful moment, but I'm really fucking cold. I stand and he scoops up the blanket, folding it into a small square. My heart races with anticipation, knowing that soon I'll have to say goodbye and watch him drive away.

We reach the cars and he turns to me.

"Take care, Ben."

It's as if he's saying farewell forever. I'll see him tomorrow, but I feel as if he's withdrawing from me and I don't get it. I stay silent.

Then he's in his car and driving away from me. I stay where I am and watch the taillights of his car until they're out of sight. A sudden shiver forces me into the car and I crank up the heat until my teeth quit chattering.

My mind does not stop spinning all the way home. Normally I would listen to some music, but tonight all I hear are the tires on the road. Once I pull into my drive, I turn off the engine. I sit there for a moment, still thinking about the past few hours.

I'm not sure what I expected. JD's an honorable man. I know that. What did I think he was going to do? Throw me on the blanket and make me forget my own name.

"Yeah. You should have done that," I say in the silence of my car.

Inside the house, I hang up my keys and jacket, and head to my refrigerator. I contemplate beer but I don't want to go down that path. I don't even know why I keep it as I don't like the taste. I pull out a bottle of water and down that instead.

I'm just heading for my bed, hoping I'm not going to spend hours staring at the ceiling, when there's a gentle knock at the door.

I reverse course and jog to the door and open it, not really surprised to see JD standing there, looking miserable. I step back and let him inside. I don't want to have this conversation on my doorstep. Some of my neighbors don't sleep too well. At least there are no lights on that I can see.

"I'm sorry, Ben. We shouldn't have left like that. I should have explained better," JD says, his voice low and contrite.

"It's okay," I say, even though it's not. "I understand why you're protecting both of us."

"I didn't want to hurt you." He steps closer to me. "You're important to me, Ben. You always have been.'

"I am?" My heart beats faster and I can feel the heat of his body, even though we're not touching.

"You always have been. I don't want to lose you," he says, his voice rough with emotion. "But I can't be with you like that. It's not fair to you. I'm your boss."

"I know that," I say, feeling a lump in my throat. "But I can't help how I feel."

"I know," he says, and then he surprises me by leaning in and kissing me softly on the lips. "I can't promise you anything, Ben. But I want to have you in my arms, just once."

"You want to kiss me?" I ask cautiously, not wanting to get the wrong idea.

"I want to kiss you, and then I'm going to go home and stay awake all night, imagining what it would be like to sleep with you in my arms."

I give a shaky laugh. "You're a frustrating man, JD."

"I know. I'm sorry."

"Just kiss me," I urge.

JD reclaims my mouth, and this time I know he means it. This is no mistake. This is no chaste brush of our lips.

I wrap my arms around him and kiss him back with a hunger I didn't even know I had. His lips are chapped and rough, and his body is so much bigger and harder than mine. He's so much stronger than I am. It should make me nervous but instead, it makes me feel safe.

One kiss melds into another and I know he won't move from this spot. He won't take me to bed as much as we both want it. We continue to kiss, our bodies pressed tightly together. I can feel his arousal growing and it only makes me want him more. I run my hands over his back, feeling the muscles tense beneath my fingertips.

He breaks the kiss, panting heavily, and looks into my eyes. "I can't do this, Ben. I shouldn't have come here."

"Then why did you come back?" My voice is raw, cracked. I can't deal with the way he swings between the sweet man kissing me and the sheriff. But they are the same people. I know that.

He gives a helpless laugh. "I don't know why I came except I couldn't leave it like that. I need you to know how I feel."

He bends his head and kisses me again. I grab the collar of his jacket and hang on for dear life.

My toes curl. Fireworks burst overhead. There are stars in my eyes. Etc, etc. Behind that dour exterior, my sheriff knows how to kiss.

When he raises his head, his eyes are hooded and I can't see his expression. But I just know he's going to apologize again or pull back or something.

I lay a finger over his mouth. "Don't say anything else. I wanted this. I still want this."

"But…"

I kiss him again. It's the only way to shut him up. It works.

7

JD

*T*he early morning is crisp, late summer leading into early Fall. I close my front door and breathe in deeply, feeling the hint of the colder weather coming. I'll need to change my tires soon. It's on the list.

The thought of the cold reminds me of kissing Ben in his hall. It didn't go further than not-so-gentle kisses but I've relived every single kiss. I left him when sanity came back to me and I remembered my car was parked in his drive. He didn't try to stop me but I saw the longing in his eyes. We both knew the risks.

Ben's not said a word and nor have I. If he'd made a complaint about me I would have deserved it. Instead he just treats me like normal, taking care of me with coffee and cannolis. He's everything I want and nothing I expect.

I huff and try to push those thoughts away. It's time for my morning patrol of Collier's Creek. Today is Jake's Day. I get to celebrate being related to the founding father of

Collier's Creek by giving a speech. I can never relax until it's all over. It's like doing the best man's speech at a once-a-year wedding. Everyone claps politely and then I can relax.

I get a burger and a soda and patrol around the Jake Collier Memorial Park, watching everyone have fun. There's some petty crime, but even the known miscreants take the day off to enjoy themselves. We keep an eye on the empty houses too. Just in case.

All the stores are dressed up to celebrate the day. It's the one day of the year Collier's Creek lets itself shine.

I stop to admire Bibi's Blossoms, Blooms & Bouquets. The florist has worked wonders this year with sashes for Jake's Day. I need to introduce myself to the new guy. Bibi doesn't stop raving about him. He's kinda young, with a weird-ass name, and more of a klutz than I am. I know he's upset a few locals with his potty mouth. I've told them to give him a break. He's from England and they're different there. Why he's here in Collier's Creek I've got no idea. But he's really good with flowers. I admire the store window again and I'm about to move when...

"No coffee this morning?"

I jump at the unexpected question, and if I'd had a drink, I'd now be wearing it.

Ben snickered. "Morning, Sheriff."

"I swear you all do it deliberately," I grumbled.

"You know we do."

"Well, not today, because I don't have more clean uniforms."

And I'm missing the caffeine like anything. But I'm determined to stay clean until after my speech.

Ben sighs and points toward CC's. "Come on, you need coffee. You'll be unbearable otherwise."

"I just explained..."

"Walk."

Please explain to me why I'm following him down Main Street like an obedient dog?

"You could have done your walk out of uniform."

I stare at him.

He sighs again. "Clearly not."

In CC's, Ben points to a table. "Sit and stay."

I glower at him. "Woof."

Of course, we're getting all the attention from behind the counter. Cameron is doing his best not to laugh at me.

Ben leans toward me and I'm uncomfortably aware he's in my space. I can smell the coffee on his breath. What must people be thinking? I try to take a step back when something shoves me from behind and I crash into his arms. We stagger, I hold him tight, and somehow we manage to keep on our feet.

"Fuck, I'm sorry, are you guys okay?" A young man looks between us. "Oh hey, Ben." Then he glances at me and takes in the badge. "Sheriff Morgan. I'm so sorry, I didn't mean to…"

He waves at me and it's only then I feel something dripping uncomfortably down my back. I close my eyes and open them to Ben's blue-gray eyes. I'm expecting him to be laughing at me. Instead, he looks angry, and I realize he's not angry at me but at the guy.

"Be careful, Wayne."

I expel a long breath. "You were right," I say to Ben.

He looks confused. "I am? I was?"

"I should have left my uniform until later."

Wayne shifts from one foot to another, only relaxing when I say "It's okay. It happens. To me. A lot."

"The sheriff is right, Wayne." Cameron leans over the counter to hand a drink to Wayne and a towel to Ben who dries me off. I feel like that dog again, but I guess I can't do it myself. I'm surrounded by three young guys half my age, and I'm the one being dried off.

Wayne mutters another apology and scurries out the door like the hounds of hell are nipping at his heels.

"If I hadn't dragged you here, you'd still be clean. This is not your fault," Ben said.

"No, it's yours," I say as cheerfully as I can muster.

His eyes widened. "Mine?"

"Yup. You can buy me a coffee and then we'll work out what I can wear to the parade."

"You need to do your laundry more often."

He scolds me like I'm a teenager and he's my mom. I give him a steady look and he flushes.

"Sorry, Sheriff."

"Ben, your order's ready."

He looks over to the counter. "Thanks, Cameron." Then he turns to me. "I was gonna suggest we sit and talk while you drink, but I guess that moment's lost now."

"Well and truly," I agree as I pluck at my shirt. "And this is just sticky."

"I think your pants are saved. It was just the shirt."

Ben goes an adorable shade of crimson when he realizes what he just said. I feel my cheeks heat too.

"Good to know," I manage.

Please God don't let anyone have heard that exchange. When I look at Cameron's shit-eating grin, I sigh and meekly accept the coffee. The sheriff's dignity is in the dirt, again.

We walk back toward my house. I'm not in the mood to patrol any further. But the coffee is hot and just as I like it, and I can feel the caffeine burning through my body.

We get a few odd looks as we walk back but mostly it's smiles. They know we work together.

Ben snorts as we reach my front yard. "What are you going to wear?"

"I've got enough button-down shirts. I'll wear one of them."

"Why don't you relax? Wear a flannel shirt like everyone else?"

"I'm the sheriff. I'm supposed to be smart. "

"Wear the badge and your hat. You'll be plenty smart and everyone sees you're having fun too."

"I'm not supposed to have fun," I grumble.

"That's bull. Who told you that?"

It was a valid question. I thought about it for a moment. "No one. It's just the way I've always been. Kinda grumpy."

He gives me the side-eye. "Kinda?"

It's his turn for the side-eye. "You know I'm your boss, right?"

Ben's sudden grin makes me want to catch my breath. "I have heard."

I can't help laughing. He makes me see the sunshine even when he's been cheeky.

"Do you want to come in?" I ask. "I can drive you home."

To my disappointment, he shakes his head. "I've promised to meet a friend for breakfast."

"Oh, okay, well have a good breakfast."

"You could join Jack and me if you like."

I couldn't think of anything more awkward than sitting with two young men. I'd look like their dad. What would we talk about?

"I need to get to work, but thanks for the offer." Do I see a glimmer of disappointment in his eyes? Maybe I'm imagining it because it's just what I want to see. "I'll see you at the parade."

Ben inclined his head. "See you at the parade. Remember fun is good."

I grunt at him and he laughs as he lopes away, back the way we came. He didn't have to walk with me back to my house. He chose to. For one moment I feel all warm and then I close my eyes. He's a young guy. He needs someone his age. I can crush on him from afar. He's not going to know my feelings for him.

It's like a mantra I tell myself all the time. Only it's getting harder to believe.

* * *

I'M MAKING notes for an upcoming meeting with the mayor when I hear Gloria screech, "It's Jake's Day."

I swear she's on the other side of the building. I wasn't expecting either of them in the office today. They'd both asked to take the day off to spend it with their families. I know I saw Ben earlier but that's different.

"Never, what made you think that?"

I smile at Ben's sarcastic drawl. The two of them have a relationship I don't understand, but it works for them. Ben has helped me to be patient with Gloria and calm her down. He's a wonderful dispatcher because he's so patient with callers. I know I won't have him forever but while I do, I'm a lucky man. He'd better train the next dispatcher to bring me cannolis. Could I put that in the job description? Maybe a change of pastry next time. Cannolis are just for Ben.

"Haha," she snarks. "Hurry up or we'll miss the parade."

"You've seen that parade your whole life. Nothing's changes. The statues get older and creepier, and the cheerleaders make me feel old."

"You don't like the cheerleaders," Gloria says.

"No, but I like their boyfriends."

"So did I, honey. And they liked me too."

"Some of them liked me," Ben says smugly.

"No. Who. You've got to tell me."

"Gloria, much as I love you, you'll tell the whole town by sundown."

I suddenly feel utterly and inexorably ancient listening to this conversation. I probably drooled over the fathers of the boys they were talking about. I had a sudden memory of one of them in particular. Yeah, I blew him behind the bleachers. Steve's a father of three now and devoted to his wife. Once he realized I could keep secrets he became a friend. I should call him sometime. Blond hair, blue eyes. It occurred to me he looked very similar to Ben. I guess I have a type. He wasn't Ben though. Ben is special.

I don't hear anything else from Ben and Gloria so I guess they've vanished into the dispatch office.

Gloria's right about one thing. Today is indeed Jake's Day and I have a job to do. A knock at the door makes me jump.

"Come on." My voice cracks. I cough and try again. "Come in."

The door opens and Ben smiles at me. "Morning again, Sheriff. I like the shirt."

I flush at his praise. I went through all my button-down shirts and ended up wearing a blue check flannel shirt.

"It suits you," he says.

Immediately my day feels better. I resist the urge to go 'this old thing.' I am a clothes horse, or I was. These days I spend most of my time in uniform. I don't go clubbing like I used to. I spend my evenings working. That's so sad. I need to pick up my phone and call a friend. If they still remember me.

Ben breaks into my miserable thoughts. "We're off to watch the parade. Do you want to join us?"

I blink at the second unexpected invitation from him. "I...er..."

His expression falls as I stammer my way toward another no.

"I'm waiting for a phone call," I finally manage to get out. "But I'll be there in time for my speech."

His smile returns if slightly dimmer. "You'd better not forget or the mayor will send me to drag you to the park."

"It was one time," I protest, "and Mrs. Masters was having a baby. I could hardly leave her husband to panic alone just so I could give a speech."

We grinned at each other, remembering the occasion. I'd been a deputy then, but did the speeches because the previous sheriff hated public speaking. I'd been just about to deliver my speech when Mr. Masters called, panicking as his wife had gone into labor. The mayor, still the same one as now, waved at me as I tried to calm the father-to-be. I'd given the shortest speech in the history of Jake's Day while one of my co-workers talked to Mr. Masters. Three minutes later I was on my way out of town to the Masters farm. The EMTs had been delayed, but we all arrived there on time, to help deliver a beautiful baby boy. They called him James Dean after the EMT and me.

It occurs to me that was over ten years ago. We both remember it but Ben had been a kid.

"I watched you that day," he says quietly. "You were so calm as you talked to him. I wanted to be you."

"I never knew that."

"You never knew I hero-worshipped you?"

I make a noise at the back of my throat. I'm no hero. I just do my job.

"You're a good man, JD. I think that's why I've always loved you."

Then he's gone and I'm staring at the closed door, mouth open.

What did he just say?

He. Loves. Me?

8

BEN

*G*loria stares at me wide-eyed as I join her and I collapse into the seat next to hers.

"Girl, what's wrong? You're the color of my gramma's sheets. Kinda gray and nasty."

"I just told him I loved him,' I whisper, "and don't call me girl, or make me think about your gramma's sheets."

I really hate being called girl. Being Gloria, she ignores the last thing I say and heads straight for the jugular.

She fixes me with a stare which should have pinned me through the seat. "You told him you love him?"

I nod.

"You told the sheriff you love him?"

I nod again.

"Why did I do that?"

She whoops, pulls me up, and spins me around until I'm dizzy.

"Stop! I'm going to hurl!"

Gloria ignores that too. "You did it. You finally found your balls and told him how you feel."

"I am so fired," I whimper.

She waves a dismissive hand. "He won't do that."

"How do you know? Look what he did to Jacobs."

"Don Jacobs was a creep. He shoulda kept his hands to himself."

I nod, because she was right. The previous clerk had a reputation and it wasn't a good one. All the women in the office were warned about him, but no one told the sheriff. Finally, Jacobs was stupid enough to corner a tech in front of the sheriff and he was out on his ear by the end of the day. The sheriff had been mortified to discover this was going on under his watch and he sent an email around saying no one should suffer any form of harassment or bullying, and to tell him immediately.

I always wondered how Ted Warren stayed whereas Jacobs was kicked out. Gloria told me it was because Jacobs had wandering hands but Ted flirts from sun up to sun down but keeps his hands to himself.

I wonder how telling your boss you love him is classified.

Gloria put her hands on her hips. "Did you touch him inappropriately?"

I stare at her, horrified. "No, I mean definitely no. I wouldn't do that. We're at work."

I have all kinds of inappropriate thoughts about JD taking me across his desk, but that's between me, the shower, and my right hand. I don't count the kissing in my hallway. That was mouth on mouth and totally consensual. Our hands didn't stray anywhere interesting.

"I know you wouldn't, hun," she assures me, thankfully not reading my mind, because she'd never let me forget it. "You're not like that. You're what my gramma calls 'a gentleman.'"

I know her gramma. She's a riot, like Gloria but ten times worse. The chances of her knowing a gentleman is zero.

What's my next move? I think frantically. "Do I need a lawyer?"

"For telling him you love him?" Gloria rolls her eyes. "If he brings it up, call it parade fever. You're overwhelmed by Jake's Day fever or something. Lie." She gives me a speculative look. "Or you could admit it's true and you've wanted to do nasty, nasty things to him for a long time."

"I'm gonna kill you," I growl. And I'm never telling her about the kissing.

"I don't think this is the best place to make that kind of threat, Mr. Johnson."

I stiffen at the sheriff's pointed comment. Gloria looks as mortified as I feel. I turn to face him. He wears an expression I can't read.

"I didn't mean—"

"He was just—" Gloria says at the same time.

JD holds up one hand and we shut our mouths.

"I'm joking too. Call it Jake's Day fever."

Our mouths drop open. He overheard our conversation. I want the ground to open me up and swallow me whole, just like it did to my Uncle Davey—allegedly.

He huffs. "I should know better than to try and joke."

"We'll all agree with that, Sheriff." Gloria agreed. "We're just not used to it."

"Thanks," he says dryly.

The sarcasm slides over Gloria's head. "We've gotta go. Come on, Ben. See you later, sir." Then she hauls me out of the office and around the side to her car.

I don't look at her or say anything until we're in the car with the doors closed. Then we take one look at each other and burst out laughing. I clutch at my stomach as I howl. Gloria's laughing so hard, mascara runs down her face.

"Oh! My! God! Did you see his face?" She only manages one word at a time, gasping and laughing and speaking impossible.

I can't speak. I'm just a heap in the seat. When I finally get myself under control, I say, "I am never gonna live this down."

"Never," she agrees. "On the bright side, he isn't gonna fire you. Or me."

I have to agree with her. I think my job is safe, but I don't think I'm ever going to be able to look him in the eye again.

* * *

THE PARADE IS FUN, full of Collier's Creek finest. It's never changed in my lifetime and it probably never will. Folks from here are like that. I get right up close to watch the sheriff give his speech. It's short and sweet and the same one he gives every year, aside from the year of the baby, and I see the visible relief on his face when it's all over. I clap along with everyone else, and I swear I see him searching the crowd, a smile erasing his grumpy expression when he spots me next to Gloria.

He wants me to be here?

I really hope I'm not reading things that aren't there. My momma always said I had an active imagination.

"Ben, at last!"

I turn to see my momma and brother. He's scowling as usual. When I turn back the sheriff is gone. I turn to smile at Momma and offer her my arm.

"Let's go have fun, Momma."

"Kill me now," Sam mutters.

"Take a deep breath," Momma says under her breath.

I smile at her. "Whatever you say. But I'll be having words with my baby brother later."

He flips me off behind her back. I huff and turn away from him because I can't return the gesture. I still don't get why he's so antagonistic toward me. We used to do everything together, but since I returned home, he doesn't want to know me.

I spot JD out of the corner of my eye. He's all alone and I wish I could invite him to join us. He catches me staring at him. I feel my cheeks heat. But he gives me a half-smile. I'm ready to run over and beg him to join me when he's approached by two good-looking guys, maybe in their thirties. He knows them, whoever they are because he's smiling and shaking their hands.

"Are you okay, Ben?"

I turn and see Momma giving me a concerned look. "Uh, yeah, why?"

"You were growling."

"Just something in my throat," I say hastily.

I hear a derisive snort behind me and grit my teeth. It's going to be a long day.

* * *

I'M tired and ready to leave after a few hours. Momma left an hour ago saying she needed to prepare dinner. I think she just wanted time to herself. I can't say I blame her. Sam lightened up when he spotted his friends and vanished into the crowd. I haven't seen him since then. I just hope he stays away from the liquor.

When Momma left I wander around the park, chatting to folk I know and catching up with high school friends. Okay, so I'm hoping to 'run into' JD, but he seems to have vanished. Maybe he's returned back to the office.

Then someone grabs me from behind. I panic momentarily until I realize who it is.

"Gotcha!" Gloria crows.

"Christ, I nearly shed my skin," I yelp, then I see Gloria's mom scowling at me for the profanity.

"Sorry, Mrs. Lester."

"It was my fault," Gloria says contritely, but she smirks at me behind her mom's back and I roll my eyes.

Gloria's mom forgives me and I spend the time with the two of them until I'm done and and make my escape, saying I need to get back to Momma.

"You come over for dinner soon," Gloria's mom says.

She holds out hope that I'll see the light and fall in love with her little girl. That's *never* going to happen. Thankfully Gloria isn't interested in me at all, and laughs every time her mom brings it up. She's gotten real good at deflecting her mom when she starts hinting.

I lope toward the exit before I have to commit to anything else, rounding the corner, to stop suddenly, surprised to find JD leaning against an aspen, his eyes closed. He must have heard me because he opens his eyes.

"Ben." He doesn't look thrilled at being discovered.

"Sheriff, what are you doing here?"

He doesn't answer immediately. I look around but he seems to be on his own.

"Uh, are you hiding, sir?"

He screws up his face. "Okay, when do you call me sir?"

"Sheriff."

"I thought we'd agreed on JD when we're off duty?"

"You're never off-duty," I tease. "And you haven't answered my question."

"Yes, I'm hiding. From Geraldine and Barky."

I snort. JD's feelings about the inseparable pair are well-known. "She probably wanted to invite you to another play-date with Barky."

"Ha ha."

69

"She *did* want to invite you on a date."

"A date with Barky," he agrees. "She thinks Barky needs more friends."

I laugh at his horrified expression. "And Geraldine picked you?"

"Don't laugh. She's deadly serious about it."

I cackle and receive the familiar scowl. "Well, you and Barky are both growly and grumpy. You could be best buddies."

"Thanks." He glowers at me.

"She doesn't like me at the moment," I confess. "She called 911 yesterday and I took the call. Barky was misbehaving."

"What did you say?"

"I recommended dog training classes."

His eyes go wide. They're the smoky blue-gray of the light off the mountains. I realize I'm staring at him and force myself to blink.

"You didn't!"

I wince. "Geraldine didn't take it well."

"I'm not surprised. You should know better."

JD is right. I should know better. Geraldine is just one of our eccentrics and no amount of suggestions about training her dog will change her.

"I won't do it again. It was a painful lesson."

Geraldine took a long time to calm down. I had to beg in the end to answer other calls.

"What are you doing here?" JD asks.

"I'm gonna home," I say. "I promised Momma I'd have dinner with her and Sam. I think she needs a buffer."

JD grunts.

"Do you want to come have dinner with us?"

I regret the impulsive offer as soon as it comes out of my mouth. I can see him building up to say no.

But he looks regretful. "I can't, but thanks for the offer. I'm having dinner up at Twisted Pine tonight."

I try not to snarl "Mine!" The handsome ranch manager, Nash, would be just his type. More suitable than a dispatcher with a stupid crush on his boss. JD will tell him all about me and what I'd said and laugh at me.

"Ben."

"Huh?"

"You're kinda growling." He looks more bemused than anything else.

I deflate. "I'm sorry, I should go."

JD reaches out and catches my wrist in his large hand. "What's wrong?"

"Nothing."

"Ben."

I hear the stern note in his voice and my cock hardens just thinking about it.

"Yessir?"

"JD."

"It's hard to remember," I confess.

He steps close into my space and I forget how to breathe.

"What do you call me in your head?" His voice is a low rumble that resonates through me.

"I don't call you anything," I mutter. "My mouth is too busy doing other things."

I swear he stops breathing too.

Then I play my last sentence back and groan. "Is there anyway I can take that back?"

He licks his lips. "What kind of things?"

"What?" Now I'm confused.

"What kind of things is your mouth doing?"

"Kissing you, blowing you. Begging you to fuck me."

His eyes grow heated and he makes that growl that makes me want to drop to my knees and beg to blow him.

71

JD shoves his hands in his pockets. "You make me want to do nasty, nasty things to you, Ben Johnson."

He's quoting Gloria's words back at me. I should be mortified. Instead I'm hard as a rock. I take a chance and glance down. His bulge is just as obvious as mine. He's as turned on as I am.

"But I'm your boss."

"I resign," I say promptly.

"You'd better not," he growls.

"I can find another job."

It would kill me to leave. I love working at the sheriff's office. It's the nearest thing I get to my dream of being a deputy sheriff.

"We need to talk," he says and he reaches out to smooth his thumb over my lips.

"When?"

"Soon," he promises.

Then he leans forward and kisses me, and time stops.

9

COLLIER'S CREEK

JD

*H*is mouth meets mine in a gentle brush of lips that's sweet and chaste and we can still step back from this. Then he walks into my space and his arms wrap around my neck so tightly like he never means to let me go. The undeniable heat of his arousal ignites sparks within me that go straight to my cock. There's no coming back.

I am his.

I'm the one playing with fire now. We're standing at the edge of the park. Anyone could walk around the corner at any moment and find the two of us in a clinch. Where's my usual caution, my professionalism?

Yet one taste of his lips and I'm throwing that to the wind. I want Ben in my arms, in my bed, in my life. Is it lust? Maybe, but I call it love.

Our bodies meet like they're made to fit together, like the wooden puzzles my dad loved taking apart and fitting back together, each piece fitting perfectly. That's how we mold together.

Ben Johnson is mine.

His lips are as soft as I remember from our kissing in his hallway, and there's just the faintest hint of fuzz on his chin. I know from walking in on a conversation at work that Ben rarely shaves whereas I look like a lumberjack if I miss a day.

I open my eyes and he's staring cross-eyed at me. It's kind of freaky.

"Why are you staring at me?" I murmur against his lips.

"Because I'm afraid if I blink you won't be here," he confesses. "You left me alone last time."

I smile against his lips and a smile curves his mouth in response. I know how he feels but I'm not going to admit it.

"This is dangerous," I say.

"One more kiss and I'll let you go."

"One more."

Like it was going to be just one. One becomes two. And three. I'm not stupid. I can't let myself go completely in case we're spotted, but Ben's kisses are addictive. I've never met anyone who tastes as good as he does.

At first our kisses are heated but still closed-mouthed, more about the closeness of our bodies than anything else. But it's not enough. I want to explore his mouth and make him mine.

Before I lose my mind, a sudden burst of laughter breaks into our moment, just as his phone buzzes against my hip.

He makes a moan as I pull away, putting space between us, and I'm ready to haul him back into my arms and throw him against the tree, waiting for me to pounce. I don't want to be sensible. I want to be a man, not a sheriff.

"Your phone," I manage as a couple, the dad wearing a sling for his baby, round the corner. They give us a curious look. I really hope we don't look like we'd just mauled each other. I can imagine the local media.

'Jake's Day shocker. Sheriff assaults co-worker."

The owner and editor really don't like me since I refused to look the other way at the editor's latest DUI.

They would revel in this story. It would run for weeks and I would be out of a job and Ben's reputation trashed. I couldn't have that. I couldn't harm Ben.

Ben smiles at the couple and coos at the baby, as he pulls out his phone.

'Hi, Momma."

Strangely enough, Ben talking to his mom seems to relax them and they walk past with a cheerful, "Afternoon, Sheriff Morgan."

When I was first elected to the post, I wasn't sure what to call myself. Sheriff Robert Charles in a neighboring county has been Sheriff Bob for years. Sheriff JD doesn't have quite the same ring and no one calls me Jeff or Jeffrey. So Sheriff Morgan I became.

"Afternoon, Rusty. Anna. How's Cherry today? Recovered from her cold?"

Anna beamed at me. "She's just fine, Sheriff Morgan."

I'm pleased to hear that and I say so. They glance between us once more and move on. I breathe a sigh of relief.

Ben finishes his call with a regretful huff. "Momma was checking up on me. I'm late. I blamed you."

I glower but secretly I'm willing to incur to incur the wrath of Mrs. Johnson. If Ben stays here any longer I won't be responsible for my actions.

He hesitates and I know he's waiting for me say something but I'm not sure what to say. The longer I leave it the more awkward it gets.

He sighs, kisses me on the cheek, and tells me we'll talk another time.

Then he's gone and I'm left touching the place where he kissed me.

"Sheriff."

I turn to see Gloria, her arms across her chest, giving me a look which should shrivel my balls or at least make them want to climb up inside my body. I resist the urge to cover my groin.

"Gloria, is everything okay?"

"You tell me."

"I'm sorry?" I don't like playing mind-games, especially not with junior members of staff. She's got a clump of mascara under her left eye, like she wiped it several times and didn't look in the mirror.

"You and Ben."

I try to ignore the fear threatening to paralyse me. From the conversation I overheard back at the office, I knew she was aware of Ben's feelings for me.

"There is no me and Ben."

"So I didn't see you lip-locked with your dispatcher? It was a figment of my imagination?"

Shit. If Gloria saw, how many others did?

She flaps her hand. "Quit panicking. Only I saw you. I came after Ben to give him a message and found you two busy. I was your guardian angel."

Just the thought of Gloria with wings is enough to make me grin. She returns it, then fixes me with a scowl to rival mine.

"You were very lucky. Geez, couldn't you have found somewhere more private for your first kiss?"

I slump against the tree and drag in a shaky breath. I didn't like to point out it wasn't our first kiss or even our second. We were just catching up. "I know it's inappropriate."

Gloria gives me the side-eye. "Half the gay guys in this town are in age-gap relationships, and have you looked at some of our parents? Yeah, it can be skeevy, but I know you. Anyone else and I might have a complaint, but you're a decent man. At least you are so far. Don't tell me I've got that wrong?"

She pauses and I realize she's waiting for an answer.

"I try to be. I don't always get it right."

I don't know why I'm trying to convince her that I'm a good man, but she's Ben's friend.

"You're a decent boss even if you do have a stick up your butt." Gloria claps her hands over her mouth. "I'm sorry, I wasn't supposed to say that."

I laugh because this is so like her. "I'll let it go, for today only."

"Thanks, Sheriff." She smirks at me, then her smile fades away. "Ben's a good guy."

"He's a great guy." The best.

"Yeah. You treat him right. Don't hurt him."

"I can't promise not to hurt him, but I'll always treat him with the respect he deserves."

Even if it breaks my heart in the process.

She rolls her eyes again. "You two are such idiots. Fuck and find out if you're compatible first."

I give her a steady look. "Before you cross another line, remember I am still your boss."

She holds up her hands and I notice her nails are decorated for Jake's Day. "Okay, okay. But Ben is my friend and I get the feeling he doesn't know much about relationships. I'm going to look out for him."

"I think you already have," I say.

"That doesn't stop just because you two have bumped uglies."

I blink. I have no idea what that means but it sounds painful. Someone calls Gloria's name and she looks over her shoulder.

"I've got to go. You take care of each other, okay?"

I nod and she vanishes back into the park. I let out a long breath, feeling as if I just dodged a bullet. I take a slow walk back to my place. I have laundry to do before I leave for my night out.

* * *

I ENJOY my evening up at the Twisted Pine Ranch. It's a relief not to have to think about Ben just for a few hours. He consumes most of my waking and sleeping thoughts. I take the twenty miles to the ranch at a slow pace, gazing at the scenery and enjoying time away from Collier's Creek. This is still part of my patch, but I don't get out here nearly enough.

The cook at Twisted Pine is a long-time friend and I enjoy his company. Burl Montgomery keeps me entertained as he cooks dinner. He and my dad had been friends for years before I was born. When my parents passed I fell into the same easy relationship with him. Not having another night of frozen dinners is also a relief and Burl can really cook.

He watches me devour his potroast with amusement. "You know, cooking ain't rocket science, JD. You could make this for yourself."

I snort at the thought. "You've seen me in the kitchen, Burl. I'm enough of a klutz with a cup of coffee. I'm a disaster waiting to happen trying to cook. Mom banned me from her kitchen after I set the table on fire."

"I told her I'd teach you after that incident. Anyone can learn to cook."

I look at Burl over a forkful of beans. "What did she say?"

"She said she wanted to stay friends with me."

I let out a belly laugh. "That sounds like my mom."

"It does," he agrees. "Teresa despaired about your ability

to survive as a adult. I said that was what frozen dinners were for."

I mock gasp and place a hand over my heart. "She must have been horrified."

Burl rumbles out a laugh. "She was. I had to apologize and promise I'd cook for you occasionally."

"Damn, that must have been some apology. You're still feeding me after all this time."

"It's what I do." He chuckles. "But maybe you've got someone else who can cook for you now?"

I stop breathing, fear gripping me. "What do you mean?" The words sound strangled as if I'm forcing them out.

But Burl just rolls his eyes. "Geez, JD, take a breath. I saw you with the Johnson kid at Randy's. It's obvious you care about him and he couldn't take his eyes away from you."

"He's too young. He works for me."

It suddenly occurs to me I didn't deny what he said.

"One you can change. The other you're stuck with. Does it matter?"

"There's plenty of folk who will think it matters," I say.

Burl shrugs. "Are you gonna let them get in the way of your happiness?"

I don't know what to say.

He reaches over and pats my hand. "You've turned into a fine young man. You take care of him, yeah?"

I scoff at being 'young' to hide my emotions and look down at my plate, not wanting Burl to see my tears. He knows, but he's kind enough to pretend he's oblivious and mentions something about checking the peach cobbler. That had been one of Dad's favorites and Burl always used Mom's recipe.

I always felt overwhelmed with emotion when we talked about Mom and Dad. Losing them both was hard and I could have been alone. I have no siblings or other relatives. But I had a close selection of friends around me, and I needed to pick up the phone more often. I didn't say it out loud to Burl. He would only roll his eyes and lecture me. Now I had someone to talk about Ben. Maybe Burl was the closest thing to family I had.

I dove into the peach cobbler with a delighted moan and we agreed the dish might be old-fashioned but it was so good. I idly wondered if Ben liked it.

We talk and eat until just after ten. I contemplate that offer of the bed because I'm so relaxed, but then it would be a really early start and I'm not a morning person despite my sunrise patrols.

I hug Burl and thump his back before I leave. "This was such a good evening,"

"You need to come here more often."

I accept his scolding with good grace. "I know. I'm sorry. Soon, I promise."

"I'll hold you to that," he warns. "And bring your man next time."

I grin, not promising anything, and head to my car, feeling full and as happy as I've been for a while. Maybe I should bring Ben out here. I cut that thought off before it starts. If I bring Ben, the ranch would know, and then Collier's Creek. My happiness slides away as I think of hiding Ben. I couldn't do that to him.

To keep me awake, I crank down the windows and blast out classic rock on my way back to Collier's Creek. I'm belting out a Springsteen number as I reach the limits of the town. My song falters as I see headlights upon headlights coming toward me. Around twenty motorcycles pass me as they ride out of Collier's Creek. It's too dark to see the riders, but what's the betting they're the same club from Gilligan's. I make a mental note to talk to Eric Kent the next day. I hadn't picked that up with him.

I slow and watch them leave in my rearview mirror. I get an uneasy feeling in the pit of my stomach. I know most bikers aren't all bad, but there's something about this particular group that sets off alarm bells ringing in my head.

I shouldn't be judgemental before I've spoken to them, but I can't help the uneasy feeling. Whatever they're here for, my gut tells me they're up to no good.

I turn my car around, intending to follow them out of town, but I lose them around a bend in the road. I don't know why they're here but this is definitely not good news for Collier's Creek.

As I drive back into town, I can feel the tension in the air. It's like a storm is brewing and the town is on the cusp of something big. I really hope that's just my over-active imagination.

10

BEN

I hug JD's kisses to me all the way back to Momma's. He'd held me like he never wanted to let me go, like we had all the time in the world, despite knowing that it's a risky game we're playing. We'd been flirting with danger, kissing out in the open like that. Yet I can't bring myself to care. I need this. I need him. I just have to convince JD we're destined to be together.

The late afternoon sun had already spread its fire across the sky, setting the horizon ablaze in a fiery mix of orange and red hues. I take a deep breath, savoring the scent of the freshly-cut grass, and a feeling of warmth and contentment fills me. For the first time in too long I love someone who loves me back. JD may not have said the words out loud, but I'm sure of it.

"You look happy," Momma says as I walk into the kitchen. She peers around me. "You didn't bring Gloria?"

"No, she's with her mom today."

The mom thing wanting Gloria and me to be together? It works both ways. Momma knows I'm gay. I've never held anything back from her…except maybe my crush on the sheriff. But I know if I declared an interest in girls she'd be over the moon. It's never going to happen, but I hate that I've disappointed her in some way.

Momma makes a noise I can't interpret and I pretend I haven't heard it.

"Where's Sam?" I ask.

"In his room. He'll join us for dinner."

He won't. The Jake's Day's parade is as much as he can take of playing happy families. I love my brother despite the fact he's an asshole. I wish I could get through to him, but he keeps his barriers up and tightly locked.

But I smile at my mom and talk about my job while I help her make dinner.

I entertain her by launching into a highly redacted–to protect the blushes of the not-so-innocent and to keep my job–funny story about a 911 call from one of the townsfolk. Some people really don't know when to call the first responders, and when to keep their proclivities secret.

"Sheriff Morgan doesn't know how lucky he is to have you," she says.

I choke on my soda at the thought of JD having me, over his desk, in the break room, in the back of a patrol car. I don't care where he takes me, I just want it to happen.

Coughing uncontrollably, tears streaming from my eyes, I reel for the sink. Momma hands me a glass of water and a towel. It takes me a moment for my chest and stomach to quit working against each other.

Momma gives me a resigned look. "I thought you learned to drink when you were little."

I flap my hand and carry on coughing, but I know my dreams are going to be full of JD Morgan tonight. He had kissed me like he meant it. Like I was the most important person in the world to him and I had kissed him back. So I couldn't stop thinking about him. I wonder if he's left to go to Twisted Pine Ranch. I grind my teeth as I think of him visiting another man, even if it is Burl. He should be with me. I run through all the guys he could be visiting. Fit, handsome men. I clench my jaw so hard it aches as I think about him in the arms of another man.

"Baby? What's wrong? You look as if you want to kill something."

Or someone.

I glance up to see my mom's worried expression. "I'm fine. Just trying to remember I can't drink and breathe at the same time."

She gives me a gentle pat on the back. We return to preparing dinner and I try not to think about what JD could be up to right now.

Wonders of wonders, Sam does join us for dinner and it's almost like the old days, settling down to watch a movie after dinner. Sam and I bicker over what to watch. He's into superheroes and I'm into action movies. We settle on *The Mummy,* the new one, and poke holes in it all the way through until Momma tells us to shut up because she likes Tom Cruise. Sam and I grin at each other over her head as she huffs and puffs.

I leave them around eleven and drive back to my place. As I reach Main Street a heavy sound breaks the night time silence. I see about twenty motorcycles rumble down the main road out of Collier's Creek.

"Huh, I wonder where they're going at this time of night."

Something worries me about this sudden appearance. We don't get a lot of biker activity. We're more of a football town. Worry tugs at me. I ran back to Collier's Creek because I was safe here. Am I going to have to run again? Will I have to leave JD and my family behind?

* * *

BY THE TIME I reach work, Gloria is already installed behind the desk.

"You're going to have to repark the tank, Gloria. The sheriff will only yell at you otherwise."

She huffs. "He might not."

I raise an eyebrow.

She huffs again.

I throw her a bone. "You make me coffee and I'll dock your car."

"Deal."

She throws me the keys. At my head. It's only my excellent reflexes that saves me from getting a unicorn horn in the eye.

"Gloria!"

"Sorry."

But she's not sorry at all. I can tell from her wicked smile.

I return to the parking lot just in time to find JD glowering at the woodie wagon. I hold up the keys. "I'll repark it."

"Someone needs to teach that girl to park. Don't they teach you these things in driver's ed?"

"To be fair, they don't teach you to drive a tank," I point out.

He growls. It's adorable.

Swiftly I back the wagon out of the space, turn it and reverse in, so Gloria can drive out without taking out an unsuspecting passer-by. I'd been that person more than once.

Then JD does the same and parks neatly next to me. "At least you can drive," he says as he gets out of his car.

"My dad taught me. It was about the only useful thing he did."

JD didn't ask any questions about my dad and I was grateful. My father had disappeared about five years ago. When Momma looked for him, she discovered he was living with his other wife and eight-year-old son. The only people she told were Sam and me. I thought he should go to jail. She said he had a young son who needed a father. The irony didn't escape any of us. Sam went off the rails and I ran away to college. None of us handled it well.

I smile at him to distract my thoughts and see his attention focus on my mouth. I lick my lips. He's riveted.

"What you do to me," he murmurs.

I want to step closer to him into his space, just like we did yesterday, but this is where we work and I can't take that risk.

"What do I do to you?" I say just as quietly.

"You drive me insane."

"Is that a good thing?"

He gives a wry grin. "It depends whether I'm trying to be JD or the sheriff."

"What are you trying to be right now?"

"The sheriff, but I want to be the man who shoves you up against this wall, drops to his knees, and blows your mind."

"I can think of other things I'd rather you blow," I tease with a wiggle of my hips so he gets the picture. "Or I can blow you."

His gaze snaps to my mouth. I chuckle softly.

JD drags his gaze away from my mouth and looks at me. "You drive me out of my mind," he says again.

"I hope so," I murmur. "I really do."

"Get into the office before I disgrace myself and become the town scandal."

He speaks more firmly this time and I know I've lost the chance to drive him crazy.

In the office, Gloria waggles her immaculate eyebrows at me as we walk in together.

"Don't get any ideas," I warn her as I drop her keys on the counter. "The sheriff was about to ream you out when I arrived."

"Uh-huh. And that was…uh…fifteen minutes ago?"

What? No! I look at my watch. It was five minutes, ten at the most.

She cackles at me. "Gotcha."

"You're impossible."

"That's me," she agrees.

I vanish into my office before I embarrass myself any further.

The morning is busier than I expect. I thought most people would be recovering from Jake's Day, but there is a steady stream of 911 calls. I know what I'm doing now and I field them to the deputies. There's been a rash of thefts overnight from the local stores. Money if they can find it, goods, liquor, cigarettes, that kind of thing. Petty theft at best, but the break-ins were quick and efficient. The store owners report little mess. Whoever the thieves were, they were pros. It made me thing of last night and seeing the bikers. I fielded those to Eric Kent. He was local to the area like me, and he was already dealing with the bikers.

When it's my break, I knock on the sheriff's door. "Come in."

JD greets me with a smile, then a scowl. "I'm kinda busy, Ben."

I'm disappointed, but I nod. "I didn't buy your coffee and cannolis this morning. Do you want me to do a run to CC's?"

"Not today."

He looks distracted and annoyed so I turn to go.

"Ben."

I look over my shoulder.

"It's not you. It's local politics. I'm no good at schmoozing the politicians."

I grin at him. "Just remember they want you to say yes."

He grimaces. "That's what I'm not good at."

"You can do it. Hey, did Eric tell you about the break-ins?"

"What break-ins?" He looks confused.

I furrow my brow. "I told Eric Kent this morning. The stores had a series of break-ins last night."

Now his confusion is replaced by annoyance. "He hasn't told me. I saw the bikers ride out of here late last night."

"Me too. Around eleven?"

"Something like that."

He'd been on the road the same time as me and he didn't stay at Twisted Pine. That shouldn't have made me as ridiculously happy as it did.

JD pulls a pad toward him. "What stores?"

I close my eyes and try to remember which ones called me. "Two restaurants, a hair salon, the supermarket. Not the florist or bookstore. They were fine."

"Okay."

"Is Kent here?"

"I think he's out. Want me to call him?"

JD shakes his head. I notice for the first time he didn't shave this morning and his beard is thicker. I wonder how soft it is. I want to run my palm against it.

"Don't look at me like that," he murmurs.

I've been as focused as he was with my mouth.

"You've got to come round to my place," I insist.

"It's a bad idea."

I want to get on my knees and beg, and then blow him, but the small part of my brain that's still functioning knows he's right. This could explode in our faces. We can't tear our eyes away from each other.

The door opens behind me, and Eric Kent walks in.

"Sheriff, I—"

He blinks as he sees me already there.

"Sorry, I shoulda knocked."

JD lets out a long breath. "Yeah, but I was gonna call you anyway." He glances at me. "Is the offer for coffee and cannolis still on the table?"

I'd rather have gotten involved with this discussion but it isn't my job.

I smile and say, "Sure thing, boss."

Eric looks hopeful and I can't ignore him. I raise an eyebrow. "Same for you?"

I've known Eric all my life. He has as big a cannoli addiction as JD, thanks to his Sicilian grandma.

He nods. "Thanks, Johnson."

I don't like being called by my surname in the office. They all do it to each other, but I've trained them to call me Ben. Eric knows this as well as the others. He does it as a power trip.

I give them both a tight smile and leave the office. I don't have much of my break left and I've got to get to CC's before it ends. I just hope they've still got my order of cannolis. It occurs to me I love my sheriff with pastries. Does he realize that? Is it too strange?

11

COLLIER'S CREEK
small town romance

JD

I've got to put a stop to whatever's happening between Ben and me. I'm the one in authority. Not him. It's down to me to be responsible.

Even now I'm distracted when I should be listening to Kent. From what I can tell the man's done nothing to chase down the MC club and now he's making excuses for not going out to the stores. Not for the first time, it occurs to me that Ben would make a much better deputy sheriff. He cares about people.

I lean back in my seat and give him a cold stare. "I want statements from every store that's been affected by the end of today and collect the CCTV."

Kent grimaces. "Let the insurance companies handle it. It's not like we're gonna find the culprits anyhow. They've long since left town."

I raise an eyebrow. "And how do you know that?"

There's a sudden wary expression as if he knows he's walking into a trap. "Well, it's obvious."

"Not to me, it isn't. Enlighten me, Kent."

"It was Jake's Day yesterday. Scumbags come into town to cause trouble."

"In which case, why didn't they commit the break-ins during the parade. Why at night?"

"The stores are closed and the street is empty."

I incline my head to show I think he made a good point and he seems to take heart from that.

"I don't think it's anything to worry about, Sheriff. It's a one-off event."

"You may be right, but I still want you to collect the statements and CCTV."

Kent is sensible enough to realize arguing with me is going to be futile. He barges out of my office almost knocking over Ben who has returned with our snacks.

"Eric," Ben calls, but Kent doesn't stop.

Ben looks at me. "Was it something I said?" he quips.

He hands me a cup and a bag with the familiar CC's logo.

"I've got to get back. Gloria's ready to throttle me because the town's heard about the break-ins and now everyone is calling."

"You don't want to upset Gloria," I agree.

We both shudder and grin at each other. It's these private moments I share only with Ben that make my day. Do I really have to give them up? The cold hard answer is yes, I do, if I'm to do the right thing by Ben and my job.

"Sheriff? Is everything all right?"

I blink as he speaks to me. "Huh?"

"You suddenly look upset."

I force a smile. "No, I'm fine, Ben. Just remembered I need to talk to the mayor. You know what he's like. He'll set JoBeth on me if I don't talk to him."

Ben laughs although from his expression he's not entirely convinced. He vanishes leaving me with my drink and pastry. I really need these. It's a been a long day already and it's not even lunchtime.

* * *

THE BREAK-INS SET Collier's Creek alight and after my talk with Daniel Hobart which I did need to do despite it being an excuse, I decide it's time I took an extra patrol. I believe in my office being visible and that's from the top down. My staff don't always agree with me but they understand it's policy. I also want to see if Deputy Kent is doing his job. There's something about his lack of action that's not sitting right in my gut. Just like last night I've got a feeling I don't like. I've learned to listen to my gut over the years. Which TV cop always talked about his gut? I can't remember, but he was right.

It also means I stay away from Ben…

"I'm going out to talk to the storeowners," I say to JoBeth as I jam my hat on my head.

She looks up and smiles at me. "Sure thing, Sheriff."

"I talked to the mayor and he'll send over a new budget proposal."

JoBeth chuckles at my disgusted tone. "You do this every year."

"He cuts my budget in half every year."

"You know that's kind of his job, yeah."

"You're supposed to be on my side," I point out.

"I don't take sides."

I sigh and she outright laughs at me. I should know I'm never going to get any sympathy from the mayor's wife.

People ask me why I have a mole for the mayor's office as an assistant. Because she's the best damn assistant I've ever had and the mayor isn't going to poach her, no matter how hard he tries.

Also, she doesn't want to work with him.

"I love my husband but I'd kill him if I worked for him," she tells me most days.

That makes me think of Ben. I'd have no problems working side-by-side with him. Maybe it's different when you actually live with someone.

"Can I bring you anything back?" I ask.

JoBeth shakes her head. "Not today, thanks. I've got a home-made lemon drizzle cake. Kathy made it for me."

There are times when it's just better to say nothing. JoBeth's daughter is the sweetest kid in the world. I love her dearly. But her cakes are like solid blocks you could use for doorsteps.

Evidently my poker expression isn't working because she huffs and sighs, then laughs. "I know what you're thinking."

I hold up my hands. "I say nothing."

"You don't need to. I can read you like a book."

I wait.

"Maybe an oatmeal cookie?" JoBeth looks hopeful.

And...

"And a yum-yum?"

We know each other too well.

The lemon drizzle cake will find its way to the trash and Kathy will never know.

I grin at her. "An oatmeal cookie and a yum-yum."

"It's a good thing I like you," she grumbles.

JoBeth is one of the few people who treats me like everyone else. I guess when you're married to the mayor, a sheriff isn't that high up the food chain. But I like it and she tells me when I'm being too grumpy. The only other person who treats me like that is Ben.

As I walk through the office, I'm aware of someone

watching me. I turn to see if someone needs me and find Ben staring at me. My breath hitches at his naked, hopeful expression. Why didn't I see that expression before? He wants me as much as I want him. He licks his lips, a nervous gesture he does a lot, and I track his tongue. I want his sweet tongue exploring my mouth, licking my nipples, and around my dick. Then I realize the two of us are staring at each other in the middle of the office and I'm having inappropriate thoughts about him. I tear my gaze away from him before someone notices. This is so dangerous.

I turn on my heel and stalk out of the office before I can something really stupid, not looking back, sure his eyes are boring into my back. I suck in a deep breath, leaning against my car until I can get my racing thoughts—and erection—under control.

I hit Main Street when I see Eric Kent coming out of one of the restaurants. His expression darkens when he sees me. My expression dares him to challenge me and make a fuss. He's sensible enough not to and turns away walking the few steps to the next store. Again, that uneasy feeling works its way through my gut.

I've never thought much of Kent as a cop, knowing he does the bare minimum he can get away with. But I've also learned that people work different ways. Ted Warren is a classic example. He flirts with everyone with a dick. We've had more than one discussion on the matter of flirting while wearing the uniform. But he's a good cop and people trust him.

I try to see the best in everyone and Kent could improve. But do I trust him? That's another matter.

I talk to all the store keepers affected and assure them we'll do our best to recover their stock. Most of them are resigned to the loss but they appreciate the sentiment. We talk about upgrading their security.

When I became sheriff a lot of storeowners didn't appreciate me talking about locks and shutters and CCTV. Colliers Creek was a small town and nothing happened. But times change and insurances companies demanded better security and they started to listen to me.

I spend a long time in the town and finally divert via CC's to pick up cookies and cake for JoBeth.

The girl behind the counter raises one arched eyebrow. "Ben's already been here, Sheriff."

"I know. This is a special order."

"Has Kathy been baking again?"

"I really couldn't say." I mime zippering my mouth and she giggles and hands over the oatmeal cookie and the yum-yum.

I know I've gotten a reputation for being grumpy but it's good to make people laugh occasionally.

Back at the office JoBeth stuffs half the cookie in her mouth and swears she will love me forever. Then blushes, inhales the cookies only to choke and splutter crumbs over her desk. I fetch her a glass of water.

"The last thing I want you to is choke," I grumble. "How do I explain that to your husband?"

"It's easier than trying to explain I've just declared undying love for my boss."

I flinch because that's too close to home.

The time away from the office has convinced me of one thing. I need to talk to Ben. To explain that I'm his boss and anything between us is inappropriate. Who am I kidding? We crossed inappropriate several kisses ago. But I have to say it to his face so he knows I'm doing the right thing.

I'm aware of the side-eyes when I tell everyone I'm leaving early. I rarely leave before nine most nights. But I leave quickly before anyone questions me.

I change into old jeans and an equally ancient blue

Henley, then ride over in my ancient Ford pick-up I've had since I left college, and park in the drive. I like his sweet one-story that was his grandmother's house. Pots of geraniums with red flowers tumbling on all sides line the porch. Ben once told me his mom takes care of them because he has two black thumbs as well as two left feet.

I'm just about to leave when the door opens and I nearly swallow my tongue. Ben is dressed in tight running shorts and nothing else. His hair is wet and water droplets pepper his shoulders and torso. I can't help raking my eyes over his lean frame. He's in fine shape. I know from conversations at the office that he goes running most days. He has pink nipples I want to lick, a fine layer of chest hair over creamy skin which tapers into a thin treasure trail dipping below his waistband. The shorts cling to his ass and thighs, framing his dick.

"Sorry," he gasps. "I was in the shower. Oh." He trails off as he sees me. "Sheriff?" Ben looks confused to find me at the top of his stoop. "Is everything okay?"

I huff, running my fingers through the bristles of my hair. "I don't know," I confess.

He blinks. "I'm kinda confused."

"You're not the only one."

"Do you want to come inside?"

Heat flares between us as he suddenly realizes what he'd just said.

I want to bury myself in him and come until my balls are dry.

He stands back and gestures inside. "Get in here before I say something else to get me in trouble."

He shuts the door and we stare at each other with the same intensity as earlier.

"I shouldn't be here," I murmur.

He folds his arms and I watch his pecs and biceps ripple and a few droplets run down his chest. "Then leave."

It's a challenge, I know. Put up or shut up.

I hesitate. I should walk out the door. I don't want to. What the hell do I do?

I haul him into my arms and kiss him with a fierce passion that doesn't take me by surprise any more. He makes a soft noise in the back of his throat, then molds against me like he's never going to to let me go. I shove him up against the wall, and push one thigh between Ben's legs. He rocks against it, moaning in passion. He's as rock hard as I am.

I feel like each encounter, from under the stars, to his hallway, to the park, to now, is increasing in intensity. If we don't come soon, one of us is going to combust.

"Need to have you, baby," I murmur in his ear, ready to slide down and blow him right here. I slide my hand over the bulge in his shorts in case he doesn't get the picture.

"Bedroom," he gasps, thrusting into my palm.

I freeze. If I go into his his bedroom, I can't walk it back, I can't pretend it's anything than it is. And I'll have to face the consequences.

Him, not me. I'll protect Ben from anything that's thrown at us.

12

BEN

I don't know what's going on in JD's head, but this time I'm not going to let him leave me standing alone in the hallway. I take his hand and lead him to my bedroom before he can run away.

"Ben, are you sure?" he murmurs when he sees the bed.

I'm never more thankful I made the bed that morning. It's hit or miss whether I remember.

I turn to face JD, my heart beating fast. "I'm sure," I whisper, pulling him closer. I can feel his breath on my neck and it sends shivers down my spine. I lean in and kiss him, hard and passionate. He responds eagerly, his hands running down my arms and then my bare back, sending sparks to my cock. I'm hard already, my cock pushing eagerly out of my shorts, and we've barely started.

We stumble towards the bed, our bodies entwined. I push him down onto the mattress and climb on top of him, straddling him. He looks up at me, his eyes stormy and full of desire, then down at the flushed head of my cock peeking above the waistband of my shorts.

I lean down and kiss him again, my tongue exploring his mouth. He moans softly, his hands gripping my hips. I can feel his arousal pressing against me and I grind my hips against his, causing him to gasp.

"Ben," he whispers, his voice hoarse with need. "I want you."

"I know you do."

That's been clear for a long time. I just hadn't seen it before.

I smile and lean down to kiss him again before I slide off him.

He scowls. "Where are you going?"

"Nowhere. You've got too many clothes on, Sheriff. Come on." I pull him off the bed.

"Not now," he says softly, and I know he's talking about his title, not his clothes.

"Get naked, JD," I order, and for once, he doesn't argue.

We get in the way of each other as he undresses, both of us anxious to get on with the action. In the end, I push his hands away, and strip him of his jeans and Henley. We laugh because of course neither of us remember his boots before I tug down his jeans. But then he's naked and my hands are all over him, stroking his nipples through his chest hair, and smoothing over his belly. He's all man, just like I imagined, and I bury my nose in his skin to inhale his woodsy scent.

JD reaches down and begins to stroke erection through my shorts, causing me to gasp. I push down my shorts and wriggle out of them, kicking them off the bed and onto the floor.

He looks down at his hand around my dick. "You're made for me." He sounds almost awed by that.

I chuckle softly, ignoring the tears prickling in my eyes. "Of course I'm made for you."

JD pulls me down onto the bed and begins to kiss me again, our legs tangled together. I run my hand down his chest, over his abs, and wrap my fingers around the base of his erection. He groans and pulls me close. I slip my hand up and down his shaft, feeling him twitch in my hand.

"If you do that, it will be all over," he warns.

JD pulls my hand away from him and rolls me onto my back. He straddles my hips, his erection pressed against mine. He looks down and begins to slowly thrust against me. I moan softly at the feel of our dicks sliding together, but it's not enough.

"I want you inside me," I insist. I need his thick shaft buried inside me until there's no space between us.

He eases back and leans down to kiss me, his mouth sweet on mine. "Patience."

I growl at him and he laughs openly.

Then I fumble and grab the lube from off the nightstand and hand it to JD. He grins and opens the cap, pouring some onto his fingers.

Our gazes lock as he slowly presses his slick fingers against my hole. I shudder and moan softly, closing my eyes.

"Ben, look at me," he murmurs.

I force my eyes open to watch him as he presses his fingers in and I pull my knees up, moaning softly. He pushes his fingers in and out of my hole, stretching me, taking his time, all the while not taking his eyes off me.

Sweat beads across my chest and he bends to lick a droplet of sweat running down my sternum.

"Now," I beg, lifting my hips up to show him what I need.

I whimper at the loss as he suddenly pulls his fingers out.

"Hold on, sweetheart," he says, reaching over to the nightstand and taking a foil packet.

Impatient now, I take it off him, tear it open and slip the condom down his shaft. I'm the one to make him shiver with need. Then I slick him up, thinking I want to feel him naked inside me, but that's a conversation for another time.

We rearrange ourselves, a pillow under my hips, him between my legs.

JD positions himself and presses the tip of his erection against my hole, pausing for a moment to look down at me. His eyes are so dark I can barely see the blue-gray.

"You sure about this?" he whispers.

I nod and he slowly begins to push himself into me. I groan and hold onto his shoulders as I feel him enter me because even with the prep, he's a big guy. He pauses when he's all the way inside me and we both take a minute to adjust.

"Ben, you feel so fucking good," JD whispers.

"Move your ass, JD," I whisper back.

He chuckles. "So bossy."

JD takes a deep breath and begins to slowly pull out, his gaze locked on me. He watches me as he pushes back into me, his eyes full of love and desire. I moan softly as he begins to thrust harder, the pleasure coursing through me, through every limb. It's not enough. I need more.

I throw my head back. "Harder, JD."

He changes his angle and begins to thrust into me harder, his fingers digging into my hips. My hands are stroking his back and I can feel his muscles flexing under my touch. I hook my ankles behind his back and pull him deeper into me, but he slows—the bastard—leaning down to kiss me, his tongue gently exploring my mouth, my jaw, my ear lobes. I moan softly and he kisses me harder. He kisses down my neck and begins to suck on my collarbone.

I groan and pull him closer, grinding my hips against him, needing to come so bad I could cry. He begins to thrust into me faster and I feel myself tensing up, balls tightening, ready to explode. I groan as I come, pulsing over our bellies, my body shivering with desire for him. I look up at JD, marveling at the intensity in his expression, and moan as I feel him come inside of me, shuddering hard until finally he lies quiet against me.

He doesn't stay like that for long. JD raises his head and kisses me, his tongue exploring my mouth. After a minute or so I pull away and lick my lips, tasting him. He slowly slides out of me and puts the condom in the trash can.

"Bathroom?" he asks.

"Opposite."

JD returns with a warm washcloth, and cleans me up. I giggle, my cock still sensitive, but he's thorough, I'll say that for him.

He disposes of the washcloth back in the bathroom, comes back to me and climbs into bed, pulling the covers over us.

"What happens now?" I ask quietly.

"Well, I'd like to stay here tonight." He sounds hesitant as if he's not sure of my reaction.

I can't think of any reason why I'd say no to him and I fall asleep in his arms, sticky and a little sore, listening to his breathing.

13

COLLIER'S CREEK
small town romance

JD

I wake slowly, feeling overly hot and something is pressing flush against me. It's like cuddling a too-hot radiator. The sheets are softer than mine, the mattress is harder than my bed, and someone is snoring, soft purring and little snorts.

Then I remember what happened the previous night.

Without opening my eyes I know where I am.

In Ben Johnson's bed.

Which means the snoring radiator is Ben. He's in my arms, his butt nestled into my groin which means as soon as he wakes up, my morning wood will be very obvious.

This isn't what I'd planned!

I came over to tell him nothing could happen between us and tumbled straight into his bed. Heat flushes through me as I remember what we did, over and over. I maybe an old guy, but he isn't and he drove me wild.

I groan as the memories play out in technicolor.

The snoring stops.

"Are you freaking out?" Ben asks, his voice small.

And he went straight to the point.

"Maybe a little," I agree because I won't lie to him.

"We don't have to do this again."

I open my eyes at his miserable yet stoic tone. It's still pitch black. I frown into the darkness. I don't like that idea and more to the point Ben is not one of those kind of guys. I've had my share of hook-ups in the past and I'm not ashamed of them, but I never want to do that to Ben.

"I'm having a total freak out," I admit, "but not for the reason you think."

"You don't want to cut and run?"

"No."

"I don't mind."

"Ben, shut up."

"Yessir." Now he sounds amused.

"Ben, I came over to tell you nothing could happen between us and that we had to be sensible."

"I know." The amusement is gone.

"Instead…"

"Everything happened between us."

"Yeah."

"Are you ashamed of wanting me?"

I haul him closer against me. "I'll never feel ashamed of you or what we did."

"But it complicates things."

I didn't expect to have this conversation in one liners in the dark, naked in bed. But maybe this was the place to have it.

"It's complicated and not everyone will be happy about it. You know that."

He grunts. "But we're going to tell everyone or keep it quiet?"

I hesitate and he wriggles around to look at me, although his expression is indecipherable in the dark.

"You don't want to tell them?" Ben asks.

I may not be able to read his expression, but he sounds unhappy, and I don't want my man to think I want to hide him.

"I do and we will. I've got an idea, but I need to talk to my boss and people in my office. I think it will work, but I need their approval first."

He wrinkles his brow. "Could you make it sound more convoluted?"

I laugh softly into his neck. "I guess it does, but Ben, I want to make us right and we have to face that."

It's the only way I'm going to have a relationship with him. Maybe it's a one-eighty on the previous night but it isn't like I hadn't ever thought about it.

"We're not the only couples and family members working together," Ben points out. "Other sheriff's offices do."

I hold him tight. "They do and they've gotten policies in place to deal with it."

I hadn't talked to them yet, but I'd looked up their policies online.

"And that's what you want to do?" The intensity in his tone tells me my answer is important. I can't fuck this up again.

"Yeah. I've been thinking about it for a while."

I hear his breath hitch. "You have?"

"I have."

He's quiet for a long time and so am I. It's a weighty thing between us in the dark of the night.

"We'll talk about it in the morning," he says.

"Yeah," I agree and press a kiss to his forehead.

But when I wake next time, it's lighter outside and time I

got up. Ben isn't snoring but he's still in my arms. I wonder if he slept at all.

"It's time I left," I say, pressing a kiss to the nape of his neck. "The gossip line will already be working."

"I don't care," he says.

"I do. Not just for me, but for you too."

"You're not the only one who's been thinking about us for a long time."

"You mean I didn't need to buy you all those cannolis?"

"I like cannolis."

He makes a disgusted sound in the back of his throat. "When we're open about our relationship, you're buying the pastries. It's an expensive habit."

"Deal." I agree because I'd do anything for him.

I need to move, to go home, but the desire to be in his arms was greater.

"I thought you were leaving," he teases me.

"I am, I will."

But instead I roll on top of him. Ben enfolds me in his arms and legs and we kiss for long minutes.

"Fuck me," he pleads.

"Always."

I want to bury myself in him and never let him go. I prepare him despite his protests that he's ready.

"I'm not that kind of lover," I say. "I need to know you're ready for me."

Ben sucks in a deep breath. "You're going to drive me crazy with kindness."

I could live with that.

But when his legs spread for me and he's writhing on the end of three fingers and his eyes roll back and what comes out of his mouth is just an endless plea to fuck him, I guess he's not thinking so much about me being kind.

"Get in me," he growls.

I do as he demands because I want to be buried to the hilt inside him. I push in and this time he's ready for me and pulls on my hips until there's nothing between us except the promise of what's going to happen.

"You feel so good," he murmurs. "You fill me to the point I can't think."

I discover my boy is very vocal about his needs and desires. He has a tendency to top from the bottom. We're going to have to work on that. I'm no Dom or anything kinky but when we're in bed, it's my rodeo.

"Fuck me!"

I think Ben has other ideas.

I fuck him for long moments, pushing in, pulling out almost to the head, and pushing in again. His mouth is wide open, his expression so focused, narrowed down to the thick, hard shaft inside him.

"You feel so good," he says again.

"I do?" I tease. "You like this?"

He nods frantically.

"You want me to do this again?"

He nods again.

"I can do that."

"For the rest of my life."

"I can do that too."

In the dark of the room it sounds like a vow, but it's one freely given. I had feelings for Ben Johnson for a long time before I admitted them to myself.

"I need to come," he begged.

"You do?"

He yanks my ass so I almost topple on top of him, losing my rhythm. I scowl at him, although it's lost in the darkness.

"You let me bring us off," I croon.

And I do, pushing us higher and higher, determined not to tip over the edge until he shaking in my arms.

"Fuck! Fuck! Fuck!" He yells so loudly they probably heard it all the way down Main Street. He grips onto my arms, nails digging in, and splatters us both with spurts of cum from his untouched cock.

That gives me the permission I need to thrust into his greedy, willing channel two, three, four times and groan as I come again, buried deep inside him.

My arms give out and I try not to collapse on top him, instead off to one side, but it has mixed success. I'm kind of sprawled over him, both of us sweaty and sticky, me panting like I've run a marathon, working through the aftershocks as I try to recover my breathing.

"That was so good," he manages.

I press a kiss dead center between his nipples. I'm beyond talking. He strokes my hair with a gentle touch I haven't felt since I was a kid. This man, barely more than a kid, treats me like I'm precious. Tears prickle the back of my eyes and I bury my face in his armpit so he doesn't see.

"JD?" He whispers my name.

I blink rapidly and raise my head. He can't see me in the darkness. "Ben."

"Don't walk away from me. Promise you won't do that."

I shouldn't make that promise, but I do. Like the fool I am.

"I won't ever walk away from you, sweetheart."

"I like you calling me your sweetheart."

"I don't think I've ever called anyone my sweetheart before," I admit.

"I like being your first in something."

There's a note of uncertainty in his voice and I hate that I put it there.

"You're my first in a lot of things, sweetheart. I've always put my love life second to my career."

"Why's that?"

"Never found the right man, I guess."

I've not gone without, but relationships have never been that important, until Ben came to work for me and I fell hopelessly in love with the sweet kid in dispatch.

"And now?"

"You're fishing." I'm not quite ready to lay my heart on the line. I don't want to scare him off.

"Maybe." Ben sounds more relaxed now, like he's teasing me.

"I've got to go," I say regretfully.

He whines but I'm firm this time and ease out of him. He hisses as I leave him.

"Are you in pain?" I ask, concerned.

"No, empty inside."

My eyes flick down to his hole and I want to bury myself back in there again. "We'll do this again soon, I promise."

"We'd better. I'm addicted to you, my sheriff."

I don't want to think about the fact I am his sheriff and this is the last thing I should have been doing. I had plans to make it right. The only thing that matters is Ben. I'll be by his side for as long as he wants me.

I clean up in the bathroom and dress. Ben pulls on a pair of sleep pants and a long-sleeved T-shirt. I like the fact he doesn't clean up immediately. I am still all over him.

He walks me to the door and we exchange lazy kisses before I open the door.

"I'll see you at work," I say. "I'll be dreaming about you all day." I wonder if that's too much, too soon, but his face lights up.

"I feel the same."

I open the door but he pulls me into the shadows to give me another kiss. As I reclaim his mouth a harsh voice disturbs us.

"Is that anyway to greet me, Ben? In the arms of another man?"

I raise my head and find a guy in black leather and a snake patch on his sleeve on the stoop, staring at the two of us, his arms crossed over his chest. I recognise the patch. It's from the motorcycle club that's been cruising through Collier's Creek.

I hear a gasp and look down to see Ben's horrified stare, his eyes almost bugging out.

"Who's that?" I ask. "Do you know him?"

"He's...he's Jarrod Stoltz."

I feel Ben shake in my arms.

"And who is he?

"Tell the sheriff who I am, Benny," Stoltz demands.

Ben pressed into me. He's really frightened of this man. I try to step between Ben and Jarrod but then Ben says three words that tear my world apart.

"He's my husband."

I let my arms fall and take a step back. "You're serious?"

Ben nods.

"That's right. Sheriff," Stoltz drawls. "The man you're holding is my lawfully wedded husband. I think it's time you let him go."

I ignore him and focus on Ben. "He's your husband? You're married?"

I want to scream "Why did you never tell me?"

"Please," he says, his expression pleading.

But I step away from Ben as all my dreams crumble into ash.

14

BEN

*S*uddenly the bikers in town and the way they'd stared at me makes sense. They'd covered their patch so I wouldn't recognize them. They were looking for *me*. I was the package. And now they've found me.

I want to run away, but I'm frozen. The nightmare from my past is in front of me. He haunted my dreams until a sweet man took his place. His dark hair is tied back in a pony tail. Hard, almost black eyes warn me I'm in trouble. I used to think he was handsome. Growing up with small-town boys, I'd always wanted a bad boy, but I'd discovered his dark side to my cost, too late to save myself.

He sneers at me. Over six foot of predator, ready to take me down. I thought I'd left Jarrod and the club behind me forever. I never told him where I lived. It was ironic really but I'd been so desperate to leave my hometown of Collier's Creek behind me, I'd made up a story about living in Vegas.

When I ran from Jarrod, I thought I was safe. But here he is, head to foot in leather and wearing the club patch. How did he find me here?

The man at my side couldn't be more of a contrast. So still, so strong, a rock. Here was real strength. Jarrod couldn't hold a candle to my sheriff.

But the only thing they both had in common was the cold, hard way they looked at me. The sweet intimacy of my night with JD was gone. His loving expression, the way I was the most important person in his life, all that has vanished. He doesn't want me anymore.

I want to beg JD to hide and protect me, but he's looking at me like I'm an insect beneath his boot.

"I need to get ready for work," he says, taking a step back.

No, don't leave me alone with Jarrod.

JD must have seen the panic in my expression because he hesitates. I beg him with my eyes not to leave me. He clenches his jaw and I see the muscles cord in his neck. He looks at Jarrod.

"You need to leave, Stoltz."

I exhale as quietly as I can.

"Not without Ben," Jarrod insists.

"If Ben wants to see you, he can do that later. He has to get to work too. You need to move on."

To my surprise, Jarrod laughs. "Whatever. I've got business to deal with. See ya later, husband. We'll meet for dinner. Don't run away 'cause I'll just find you again." He gives a derisive laugh and heads for his bike.

I don't breathe again until I see him ride off and turn at the intersection.

As Jarrod rides away, I feel a sense of relief wash over me. But it's short-lived as I turn to face JD. His expression is unreadable, but his eyes are cold and hard. No, not hard. Devastated.

"I need to go."

I flinch at JD's stoic tone."I'm sorry," I say, my voice barely above a whisper. "I didn't know he was going to show up."

JD doesn't respond, just continues to stare at me. I feel the weight of his gaze on me, and I can't help but feel like I'm being judged. This is unfair! I want to explain everything to him, to tell him about my past and how I never wanted any of this. But I know that he won't understand, that he'll just see me as damaged goods.

"Please," I say, my voice shaking. "Please don't be mad at me."

JD sighs and rubs his hand over his face. "I'm not mad at you, Ben."

But he is. I can tell by his closed expression.

"We need to get to work," he says.

"Please." I hold out my hand but he takes a step back.

"Go to work. Call the office if Stoltz gives you any problems."

"I'll call Eric."

His face tightens. "I need to go."

"JD. Sheriff. We need to talk."

"I have to get to work."

And he stalks away to his car.

I don't know what to do. I sit down on the steps of my stoop and watch JD drive in the opposite direction to Jarrod. What happens if Jarrod is waiting somewhere for me? I shower and change in a state of panic, but when I drive to work, I don't see a motorcycle anywhere. The streets are empty.

JD is already at the office when I arrive, his patrol vehicle squeezed in next to Gloria's car.

I drag in a relieved breath when I cut the engine and rest my head on my forearms for a few minutes, trying to calm the hell down.

JD's door is closed. Today is not a day for loving with pastries. I close the door to the restroom behind me and lean against it.

"What am I going to do?" I say to the empty space.

But it doesn't answer me back.

* * *

I HOPED it would be busy so I'd be distracted, but no one seems to need help. Gloria wanders in and catches me staring into space.

"You've got to talk to him," she says, an arm around my shoulders.

"Jarrod is the last person I want to talk to."

She furrows her brows. "Who's Jarrod? I meant Sheriff Morgan. You need to talk to him."

I stare at her. Does she know about last night? How can she know? I was sure no one else saw us, even with Jarrod turning up.

"The sheriff looked like hell when he arrived this morning." Gloria fixes me with a stare that skewers me to the seat. "And you look like someone's kicked your puppy. Talk to me, Ben. Did something happen between you? Did he hurt you? I'll kill him." Her tone is fierce and I'm glad she's on my side.

"He didn't hurt me, Glor." I have to intervene before she stamps off to shout at JD. "It wasn't him. JD would never hurt me."

At least not physically. He'd stamped on my heart but he'd never use his fists on me, I was sure of that.

"Then who was it?"

I expel a deep breath. "It was Jarrod."

"Who's Jarrod?" She repeats the question.

"One of the bikers."

Her plucked eyebrows shoots up almost comically. "You know one of the motorcycle gang?"

I nod miserably. "He's the president of the club."

"Ben…"

"And my husband."

"Holy fucking meatballs." Gloria's jaw drops.

I wait for her to recover. She takes her time. She opens her mouth and shuts it at least twice before she finally says, "You're married?"

To give her credit, I'd expected her to screech it out to the office and this was more of a fierce hiss.

"Yeah."

"What the heck? Does the sheriff know? More to the point, does your momma know? She's going to kill you."

"I know," I say miserably. "She doesn't know yet. JD does."

I bite my bottom lip. From the way her eyes go wide, Gloria spots my slip.

"How does he know?"

"I'll tell you, I promise, but I need to talk to Momma. I'll go after work."

"You go now. You know what the town gossip is like. I've finished my shift. I'll cover you to the end of yours."

"You can't do that."

"Yeah, I can." She tries to manhandle me out of the seat.

I flap my hands at her. "Get off me."

"Then shift your butt. You need to talk to the sheriff about leaving early."

"I can't—"

"You can."

"You should be the sheriff. You're so bossy," I mutter.

"It's on my things-to-do list," Gloria assures me. "And don't call me bossy."

I open my mouth but there's a call and she takes my seat with a triumphant wave toward the door.

My feet are like lead as I approach JD's office. I knock on the door, but there's no answer.

"The sheriff's gone to Huntersville," Deputy Aimee says from behind me.

I glance over my shoulder and give her a wan smile. I like Aimee. She doesn't treat me like an idiot.

"Wow, you look rough. Are you sure you're not going down with the same thing Sheriff Morgan has?"

So the thought of going down on JD momentarily distracts me, but she continues. "Do you need to talk to him?"

"I'm not feeling great," I confess. "Gloria says she'll cover the end of my shift. Is that okay?"

"Sure. You go home and rest." She pats my shoulder, and I smile at her and make my escape.

* * *

GLORIA'S RIGHT. I've got one place I need to go before the town gossip reaches her.

Momma's face lights up when she sees me on the doorstep. "Ben, what are you doing here? Aren't you supposed to be at work?"

"I left early, Momma."

She furrows her brow. "Why? You don't want to get a reputation for slacking off." Her gentle scolding is normal. Momma has always believed we should have a strong work ethic. Somehow that never applies to Sam.

"Momma, can we talk? I've got something to tell you."

"That sounds serious," she says, grinning at me, but it fades away when I don't return it. "Come sit down. Sam's not here."

That was mom code for he's getting liquored up somewhere, but right now, my brother getting drunk isn't top of my priorities.

We sit at the kitchen table. I'd spent most of my family life around this table, eating meals, playing with my toys, later on doing homework. Momma had always believed the kitchen was the heart of the family.

Now she looks at me, her expression worried. "Sweetheart, tell me what's wrong."

I wince at her opening word. I'd treasured JD calling me his sweetheart, but he'd never call me that again.

"Ben?"

"I've got something to tell you," I say again.

I see the worry in her eyes and I suddenly realize what she thinks I'm trying to tell her. "I'm not ill, Momma. I promise."

She sucks in a loud breath and gives a shaky laugh. "Okay. Okay. That's good. So what are you trying to tell me?"

"When I was away at college, I did something stupid."

"You dropped out of school. That's okay. College isn't for everyone."

I've heard all this from Momma before. She'd been disappointed but never told me I'd let her down. Now I need her to listen to me but how do I tell her what a total fool I made of myself? "I met someone."

"A girl? Is that why you left college. Did you make her pregnant?"

I huff at the disapproving tone and the words because Momma knows I'm gay. She doesn't hassle me, but I know she keeps hoping one day I'll bring home a nice girl. "No, Momma. I'd never do that to a girl. And it was a man."

"Okay." One word, telling me she's disappointed but she loves me and wants me to be happy. "Why is that stupid? Meeting people is what you're supposed to do when you're at school."

I lick my lips. "I married him."

She gives a slow blink as if it's taking time to process the information. "You got married?"

I nod.

"To a man?"

Another nod.

"And you didn't tell me?"

Now I've hurt her, I can tell. Momma once told me her only regret for having two boys is that she'd never get a chance to plan her daughter's wedding. She said it lightly and with love, wanting us to know it was a minor regret and she loved us. I'd told her then she could help plan my wedding. She'd laughed and said my bride would have something to say about that. That was before I realized that I only liked boys and maybe one day I'd have a groom by my side.

Now I'd taken that chance away. But I have to get through the rest of the tale.

"Momma, I didn't say anything because I ran away from Jarrod."

She frowns at me. "You didn't stay and work it out? That's not like you, son. You know what I said about working through your troubles."

"It wasn't like that. I never wanted to get married to him."

"Then why did you?"

What do I tell her? "It just happened."

"And now he's found you," she says, beaming at me. "You can make up with Jarrod. It was meant to be."

"No, Momma. It's not like that. I left because—"

She cuts me off with a wave of her hand. "When are you going to bring him around to introduce me to my son-in-law?"

I shake my head, but she just glares at me.

"Benjamin Aaron Johnson. You will introduce me to... Jarrod, was it?"

I don't say anything because I know the futility of trying to argue with my mom. But hell will freeze over before I let Jarrod anywhere near my family. No one hurts my momma and brother. No one!

15

JD

J crawl through the day, hiding in my office and refusing to talk to anyone. Ben turns up late and hides in his office too. He doesn't come near me, not that I expect him to, but I miss his warm smile.

Gloria keeps giving us worried looks. I know she wants to ask me what the hell I did to her friend. I'm amazed the gossip hasn't reached her yet.

Look, Gloria, you don't need to worry about your friend. He's already married.

I know that's petty, but dammit, I'm feeling petty right now.

I'm relieved when I get a call to Huntersville on the other side of the county. Any of the deputies could have taken it but I'm desperate to get away from the office, and I'll return when I know Ben will have gone home.

When I return, Aimee catches me before I can escape into my room.

"Ben was feeling rough today. Gloria covered the last part of his shift."

I grunt. It's what I expect of my man. He never leaves without cover. Just thinking about him makes the knot in my stomach tighten.

She narrows her eyes at me. "You still look rough too. Are we all going to come down with a bug?"

"I hope not."

I'd taken my office through the pandemic and that was *not* fun.

I leave late into the evening and spend the night on my porch, wrapped in a blanket my mom knitted. If I sleep, it's for a few minutes at a time. I watch dawn break, my eyes feeling like sandpaper every time I blink. The sky changes colour from indigo to pale blue, then streaks of mauve and pink stretch across the sky. As the sun rises, I get up from the porch and stretch my aching limbs. The night had been long and restless, and I can feel the cold and fatigue seeping into my bones. I shuffle back into my house, the floorboards creaking beneath my feet. I feel a hundred years old.

"Next time, you do this inside. You're too old for nursing a broken heart in the cold."

I make my way to the kitchen and put on a pot of coffee. The sound of the water boiling and the aroma of fresh coffee beans fill the room. The warmth from the stove slowly eases the chill from my bones. I pour myself a cup and sit at the kitchen table, staring out the window at the world waking up.

What did I think would happen? Ben would fall into my arms, the town would cheer, and we'd live happily ever after? Those were the fantasies from the romance novels my mom used to read.

Except he *had* fallen into my arms. The previous night

had been magical. Everything I'd wanted and nothing I'd expected.

But now, in the light of day, reality hits me like a ton of bricks. Ben is married, and no amount of magical nights can change that fact. I take a deep breath and try to think of a way out of this mess. I can't keep ignoring Ben, and I can't keep pretending that everything is okay. I need to talk to him. How had he married the president of a motorcycle club?

First, I need to do my morning patrol of the town. I won't hide. I won't be chased away from the town I love. I dress in my uniform, and leave a fresh one out on my bed.

I stare at myself in the mirror and wish I hadn't. I look awful and my hair is a mess, my eyes are puffy, and there are dark circles underneath them. I splash cold water on my face and try to shake off the exhaustion. It's time to face the day.

I step out of my house and start my patrol. The town is quiet in the early morning, and the only sound is the crunching of the gravel beneath my boots. I walk through the streets, checking on the shops and the buildings. Everything seems to be in order. The sun is starting to rise higher in the sky, and the town is slowly coming to life.I stop to look in the bookstore window for something new to read. I have as big a book addiction as a coffee addiction, as Logan who works in Ellis Books tells me all the time. Then I head toward CC's for a coffee, because I'd been so wrapped up in my own thoughts, I'd forgotten to pour a coffee for my patrol.

As I enter CC's, the bell on the door jingles and I'm greeted with the warm aroma of coffee and freshly baked pastries. The place is bustling with people, and I spot Gloria sitting in a corner booth with a cup of coffee and a book.

I frown, Gloria is never here this early in the morning. What is she doing here?

She looks up, spots me, and waves me over.

I hesitate, then I realize I'm holding up the line. I get my coffee and stomp over to her.

"Gloria," I say, taking a seat opposite her.

"Boss," she replies. "You look like shit."

"Thanks," I say dryly.

She seems to miss the sarcasm because she nods, her eyes filled with concern. "Listen, about Ben..."

I wait for her to speak.

"What the heck did you do to him?" she snaps.

I gape at her. Me? What did I do?

"I did nothing," I hiss.

"Except break his heart. I told you to take care of him."

It's my heart that's shattered into a million pieces. I glower at her. "His husband turned up."

She waves it off like it's unimportant. "Jarrod's as much his husband as I am."

I stare at her, not sure what to say.

She leans forward. "He ran away from Jarrod. Did you know that?"

"I know nothing about Stoltz. Ben's never mentioned him."

"And why do you think that is?"

I shake my head. "I don't know."

She huffs at me impatiently, as if I'm being deliberately obtuse. "Because Ben's trying to forget his past with Jarrod."

"What are you getting at?" I ask, feeling frustrated and exhausted.

"Ben went through a lot with Jarrod, Sheriff. He's been in some dark places. He's been hurt, and it's not just physical."

"He was abused?" I stare at her in horror.

"Yeah and he's fragile, and you know that."

Gloria was right. I had always known there was something vulnerable under that sunshine exterior.

"And now he's hurt again," she snaps.

"That's not my fault." I say defensively.

She raises one eyebrow and I feel like I want the earth to open me up and swallow me whole. How does she have this effect on me?

"I left when Jarrod turned up. What else was I supposed to do?"

"Did you tell Jarrod to ride out of town and never return?"

I shake my head, feeling guilty. I had been so wrapped up in my own feelings, I hadn't even considered how Ben was feeling.

"You promised to be by his side forever and instead you ran away."

Her voice rises and I see people looking our way. I don't ask how she knows all that. Ben would have told her.

I lean forward and she mimics me. "I'd just told him I loved him and he springs an unexpected husband on me."

"I don't think it was intentional," she says sarcastically.

"Why has he never talked about Jarrod?"

"I don't know," Gloria admits. "But as I said, I think he's been trying to forget Jarrod exists."

I scratch at the stubble I didn't remove this morning. Ben and I need to talk. Even if there's no future for the two of us, he can't go back to an abusive man. I can help with that.

"I'll talk to him," I say. "I can help with the husband issue."

Even saying it out loud sounds bizarre.

"You'd better," Gloria replies, before getting up and leaving.

I sit there for a moment longer, sipping my coffee and staring out the window. No one approaches me this morning, even Will who always talks to me. It's like there's an invisible forcefield around me. The gossip has already started.

The morning sun is starting to warm up the town, and I can hear the sounds of people starting their day.

I finish my coffee and head back to my office. It's time to face Ben, and try to make things right. Whatever that may entail.

* * *

IN THE OFFICE I head for dispatch. I know Ben's on the early shift today. I know all his shifts. I poke my head around the door.

"Mr. Johnson, please come to my office."

I see Ben flinch, but he nods. I don't wait for him. I need a moment in my office before he joins me.

I stare out of my window, watching vehicles flash past, on their way to disgorge their drivers and passengers to however they fill their days.

There's a tentative knock at the door.

"Come in."

Ben enters the office. He looks terrified.

I point to the seat in front of my desk. "Sit down, Ben." I take my seat and look at him. "We need to talk about Jarrod."

Ben gives a tight nod. His eyes are downcast, and I can tell he doesn't want to talk about it. But we need to have this conversation. For his sake.

"I...I don't know what to say," he finally speaks up. "I never wanted you to find out about Jarrod. It's not something I'm proud of."

"I understand that, Ben," I say, trying to sound as gentle as possible. "And I'm so sorry for how I left you. I was shocked, but there was no excuse to leave you like that. I'm so sorry."

Ben presses his lips together and nods. He looks ready to fall apart.

"I need to know what happened. And I need to know if you're safe."

Ben looks up at me, his eyes filled with fear and uncertainty. "I ran away from him, Sheriff. I'll never be safe."

"I'll keep you safe," I promise. "How did you get involved with a member of a motorcycle club?"

"I met him at school. I thought he was exciting and fun at first, but I soon realized he has a darker side. He wanted me to marry him. I said it was too soon, but he's very persuasive."

More like coercive, I think, but I keep my thoughts to myself. I want to hear from Ben.

"I didn't know he was abusive until after we married. One day he hit me." He runs a fingertip down a thin scar near his hairline that I hadn't noticed before. "I thought, that's it. If I don't leave he's going to kill me. When he was asleep I escaped and returned to Collier's Creek. I told Momma I dropped out of college and came home. She was disappointed but helped me get a job here."

And he'd stuck to that story until Jarrod found him.

"He didn't know where you lived?" I ask.

Ben shakes his head. "No, I didn't tell him. I was too scared in case he went after my family."

I nod, understanding the fear that can come with being in an abusive relationship. "Do you want me to help you get a restraining order against him?"

Ben looks up at me, his eyes shining with tears. "Yes, please."

I reach over and give his hand a reassuring squeeze. "I'll take care of it. And I'll make sure you're safe."

"Thank you," he whispers.

I force a smile. "We'll talk later."

He nods and leaves the office.

I expel a long breath. It's been a long day and it's only just started. I need to talk to a judge about getting a restraining order. And I need to talk to Kent about the bikers. We should have had more information about them before it got to this stage.

I scrub my hand through my hair. It's getting too long. I expel another breath. I just want to go home and forget this day ever happened.

16

BEN

*I*t's another hellish day. JD spends it in his office again after our talk. I haul Gloria into the dispatch office when I leave his office.

"I told you not to interfere," I hiss at her.

She waves it off like it's unimportant. "Someone had to."

"I was going to talk to him."

She gives me that "Uh-huh," look she's perfected over the years. "When?"

I say nothing and she sighs.

"He's devastated, Ben. I've never seen him look like that. I feel like I could give him one poke and he'll fall into a million pieces at my feet."

I have to swallow around the lump in my throat just thinking about it.

"He really loves you," she says, and I can hear the amazement in her voice. "You've got to fix this."

"How?"

"Feed him coffee and cannolis. Do something. I want my grumpy sheriff back."

I scowl. "He's *my* grumpy sheriff."

"Not now he's not. He's a man trying to pretend he doesn't have a broken heart." Gloria takes my hands and pulls me into a hug which almost yanks me off my seat. She ignores my protest. "You've got to deal with this, Ben, because he doesn't know what to do."

"You think that?"

"I know that."

I take a deep breath. "I'll go see him again tonight."

But when I leave the office, JD is out and he doesn't return all day. I leave, defeated, and drive home. I'm not surprised to find Jarrod on my stoop when I get home from work.

I can't avoid him for ever. But he can say his piece, then leave. I'm never going back to him. I have something better right here. If JD forgives me.

"How did you know where to find me?" I want to know the answer. I was so careful never to let him know where I lived when I was at college.

"The sheriff told me."

"What?"

My blood runs cold. That can't be right. JD would never give away information like that and he never knew about me and Jarrod.

"Yeah, Kent is it?"

The knot in my chest eases a fraction. It isn't JD. He would never do that to me. Then I take in what he just said. "Eric Kent?" I stare at Jarrod in disbelief. "He told you about me? How? He didn't know I was married to you. I've never told anyone."

"Of all the coincidences," Jarrod continues. "I met him online. We do business together. I've been searching for you,

129

and all the time you and he were best buddies."

Best buddies is a stretch but I need him to keep talking.

"Why were you looking for me?"

His eyes harden. "I want what's mine. And that's you."

"I was never yours. Never."

"You married me. That makes you my property."

I knew he believed it. I'd seen the way his MC treated its women. I'd be no different in their eyes. I wasn't a member of the club. I was owned by one of them.

This is why I'd run back home in the dead of night so he couldn't find me.

"I sent you divorce papers."

"I ain't divorcing you. Say your goodbyes to your friends and Momma. She really likes me."

"You went to her house?"

His smirk is enough.

I'm going to kill Eric Kent. And then I'm going to raise him up and kill him again.

"You're coming back with me," Jarrod says. "I'll be back in a couple of days. Me and the boys are gonna complete some business first."

Jarrod leers at me, letting me know what kind of business he means, and saunters out of my house as though he owns the place and everything in it.

There's only one thing he wants.

He stops and turns to me before he heads to the Hog. "Don't try and run. I'll only find you again."

I hear the threat.

"You're not going to have me!"

I say the words out loud, hoping, praying, that will make them true. I'm not going with him, no matter what he says.

First, I need to talk to JD.

* * *

I DRIVE BACK to the office, not surprised to find JD's car still in its parking space. He never leaves early most evenings.

I'm suddenly nervous and not sure I want to talk to him.

"Come on, you can do this. He's not gonna eat you."

"Not unless I ask nicely."

I can make crude jokes along with the best of them, as long as it's out of my Momma's hearing.

"Should I be worried about that smirk?"

JD leans against the doorframe to his office, a quizzical expression that just makes my heart turnover. Gloria is right. He looks wrecked.

"I was thinking about you doing dirty things to me," I admit.

I did check no one was in earshot before I sat that, but the hungry need followed by panic that crossed his face would have been funny if I felt like laughing.

"There's no one else in the office," I assure him.

JD is in my space in seconds. "What's wrong?"

It makes my chest tighten that he can see how upset I am even through the jokes.

I place my hands on his chest. "That obvious, huh?"

He places his warm hands over mine. "Tell me."

"Jarrod was on my doorstep tonight. He's insisting I go with him as I'm his property."

JD's expression darkens. "He said that?"

"Yeah. Over and over. I've got two days to say my good-byes, then it's goodbye Collier's Creek, and hello, disgusting hellhole." I try to sound light and cheerful, but I'm screaming inside.

JD does exactly what I need, gathering me into his arms and holding me as if he'll never let me go.

"He can't take you away."

I really hope that unspoken 'from me' is not just my fevered imagination.

"There's something else."

"Go on."

"He says Eric Kent told him about me."

I feel the tension flood through JD and he takes a step back, although he doesn't let me go.

"That's a strong accusation to make about a cop," he says, the lines between his eyebrows deep.

I shove my hands in my pockets. I know it's the last thing he wants to hear, but he has to listen to me. "Jarrod says they met online. Eric told him about me and Jarrod put two and two together."

"Fuck!" JD runs a hand through his hair, making it stick up everywhere.

I step close and smooth it down. JD makes a rumbling sound, almost like a purring cat. He likes having my hands on him just as much as I like touching him.

"You make me lose my mind," he mutters. "And I need to think."

I lean forward and kiss his cheek, then step back and give him space. "Why would a deputy sheriff be in contact with an MC with ties to drug trafficking.

"You know this?" JD says sharply.

"I do. And before you ask, I did tell the cops about Jarrod before I left him and no one listened to me."

I'd swiftly realized the cops back in Oregon had ties to the MC. I'd always thought JD was different.

He presses his lips in a tight line. "Leave this with me." He must read the doubt in my expression because he says, "I *will* investigate Kent and that's a promise. I'm not gonna sweep this under the carpet. I don't allow dirty cops in my office. But I need you to be careful, Ben. You've got Jarrod threatening to kidnap you. I should get you out of here, and find you somewhere safe to stay.

I shake my head. "I can't leave town. What about my momma and Sam?"

"Then you'll come back to my place tonight and we'll go to work at the same time tomorrow. Jarrod isn't going to get near you."

"So it's life as normal," I quip. "Despite the psycho husband and dirty cop?" He opened his mouth and I swiftly add "Alleged dirty cop."

JD groans. "You know I love my life as a quiet county sheriff living in a small town, yeah? I'm not really into high-stakes danger."

"Nor me. It just seems to find me."

I wrap my arms around myself and he must realize that, despite the joke, I'm upset, because he enfolds me in his solid embrace. I lean against him for a long moment.

"I'll protect you, I promise." The words brush my ear.

I nod and stay buried against his chest.

The moment is interrupted by my phone vibrating in my pocket. I pull it out and sigh. "It's my mom."

I don't think I'm supposed to see her tonight. We'd made plans for me to take her shopping at the weekend.

"Hey, Momma, what's up?"

"It's Sam." Her voice cracks and she's obviously close to tears. "We had a fight at dinner and he stormed out. I haven't seen him since."

JD raised an eyebrow.

"Sam. Missing," I mouth.

He nods and moves away to talk in his radio. I know he's putting a call out to the deputies on patrol.

Knowing my bro, he's getting drunk somewhere. I'd tried to cut off his alcohol supply but someone keeps buying him booze. I think where he could be. The bar and the grill wouldn't serve him. JD had made sure of that. Sam was banned from all the places that served liquor.

"I'll find him, Momma. Don't worry."

She sniffles in my ear. "You're a good boy. I don't know where I went wrong with Sam."

I had an idea but it wasn't something she wanted to hear and I'll never tell her.

"I'll call you when I've found him."

I say goodbye and look at JD. "Want to help me hunt down my delinquent brother?"

"Goody," JD deadpans, and I laugh at his lack of enthusiasm.

Sam hates the sheriff and I had a feeling the sentiment is returned. My little brother needs to get his head out of his ass, but nothing is going to convince him to quit drinking. He needs rehab, but Momma is resistant. She thinks Sam will wake up and see the light. I'm not convinced.

JD's radio squawks into life.

"Sheriff, it's Kent. Someone's kicking off at Randy's because they wouldn't serve him. It sounds like the Johnson kid."

The last thing I want is Eric anywhere near my brother. Sam's a stroppy teenager and easily manipulated, especially when he's liquored up. If Eric or Jarrod gets their claws into him, he'd believe all their lies.

"Want me to bring him in?"

"No, I'll deal with it. Thanks, Kent."

I let out a breath.

JD looks at me. "Let's go yell at your brother."

"Great. He's gonna be so pleased to see us."

* * *

I HEAR the yelling as soon as we get out of JD's car.

JD grimaces at me over the vehicle. "He's got a set of lungs."

"Momma says he'd make a great opera singer."

"Can he sing?"

"Not a note. But he can yell." I smirk at JD who snorts.

"Let's go retrieve your brother before Randy fillets him, rolls him in breadcrumbs, and fries him, in frustration. I'm going in first."

"He isn't going to shoot me."

But JD gives me a steady look and I roll my eyes and nod. "You go in first."

I blink at the dim light as I step into the bar. Then I hear Sam cursing as he spots JD. He hasn't spotted me yet.

Sam turns on Randy. "You called the cops on me?"

"Not me, but I'm sure glad to see you, Sheriff. I've been trying to explain to Mr. Johnson that I can't serve him because he's underage." The sarcasm drips from his voice. "He seems to think I'm mistaken."

JD nods and turns to my brother. "Sam, you know you've been banned from here."

"You made sure of that," Sam hisses.

"Yeah, I did. And you know why."

"So I've gotten drunk a coupla times."

"You shouldn't be getting drunk at all, but you have an alcohol problem, Mr. Johnson."

"I don't."

"You do. But right now, I want you to come with me."

Sam postures and sneers. "You gonna arrest me for trying to get a drink?"

"No, we're going to take you home."

"We?"

Trust Sam to notice that. I step out of the shadows. He sees me and his upper lip curls.

"You brought my perfect brother? What? Too scared to arrest me yourself?"

What the heck? Does Sam want to get arrested?

And then I realize that's exactly what he wants. Getting

arrested means he has bad boy cachet. Whereas right now, the sheriff brought his big brother to take him home.

JD squeezes my bicep. I see Sam's eyes narrow at the gesture. Despite what everyone thinks, my brother isn't stupid. That's what makes it so frustrating. He's so much better than this. He was a straight A student until he went off the rails.

"Ben, take your brother to the patrol car," JD orders. "Any trouble, you have my permission to cuff him."

"Yessir. Sorry, Randy. It won't happen again."

Randy gave me a lazy salute. "No worries, Ben. See you in here soon?"

If I'm still here to enjoy it.

"Looking forward to it," I say and I haul Sam out by his arm.

Sam yanks out of my grip when we're outside. "What the hell are you doing here?"

I think about following through on JD's orders. Yeah, I know how to cuff people, thanks to the sheriff's training. But I cut my brother a break, for now. "Momma called me. She said you got into a fight."

"She didn't have to call you."

"You didn't come home. She was worried."

Sam stares down at his Converses. I squint at them. I'm sure they used to be mine. "She doesn't care."

"You know that's not true," I snap.

"Whatever." He waves a hand. "I'm gonna take off now."

"No. You get in the patrol car."

He sneers at me. "Gonna make me?"

"Yes."

Sam blinks for a moment. "You gonna cuff me?" He sounds almost excited at the idea.

"Just get in the car," I say wearily, avoiding that question. "The sheriff is coming out."

Sam huffs and climbs into the back of the patrol car. He might challenge me but he really doesn't want to challenge the sheriff. "I can't believe you called the cops."

"I was already talking to him when Momma called," I say without thinking.

His eyes go wide but before he calls me on it, JD slings a bag in the trunk and gets in the car, scowling at Sam.

We ride in uncomfortable silence back to Momma's house. She cries at Sam's safe return. He yells at her to quit fussing and storms upstairs. I just want to get out of there.

I sigh with relief as we get back in the car.

"You can take me home," I say. "I'm sure you've had enough of my family today."

"You're coming home with me," he insists. "We'll go to your place to get you a change for tomorrow and then we're going to sleep."

"You haven't eaten. Neither have I," I admit ruefully.

"Dinner from Randy's in the trunk."

I'm not ashamed to say I whimper.

An hour later, we tumble into JD's warm and comfortable bed after stuffing our faces with fried chicken. His arms are around me in seconds and I nestle back against him, reveling in his solid strength.

"Jarrod is gonna sign those divorce papers real soon," he mutters.

I smile, but then it fades as I think of Jarrod's threats. I can't lose this, my sheriff, just as I've found him. I hold on tight to JD's arm.

"I got you, honey. I got you," he murmurs sleepily.

"I know you have." And I turn my head to kiss his fuzzy chin.

17

COLLIER'S CREEK
small town romance

JD

*W*aking up with Ben in my arms makes me think we can have a future. I lie for long minutes listening to him breathe gently, his warm breath sending goosebumps over my chest.

I don't know how we're going to deal with Stoltz but first we need to talk to an attorney. Stoltz is dangerous, I know that, and I don't really know how Ben had gotten entangled with him, but we have to sort it out legally.

And now I have another problem. I need to deal with one of my own. Eric Kent. Dammit. I need help and there's only one person I can think of.

I trace a light pattern on Ben's back and he sighs and snuggles close to me. We didn't do anything beyond a kiss the previous night, but having him in my arms feels right. I kiss the top of his head and he presses his own kiss into my chest hair.

"Morning."

"Morning, sweetheart."

The endearment escapes me before I can hold it back and I apologise immediately. "I'm sorry."

"Don't be sorry. I like you calling me your sweetheart."

"You don't think it's too girly?"

"Not at all."

Ben snuggles against me, sliding his leg over my thighs so that I'm trapped, his morning wood making me think of things I don't have time for.

"I should get up," I sigh.

"It's time for your morning patrol," he says. "You need to get your replacement coffee from CC's and change your uniform again."

I huff and he laughs.

"You should stop daydreaming about me."

I stiffen and he raises his head, smirking down at me.

"Seriously, you're thinking about me?"

"All the time," I confess. "Morning, noon, and night. I can't stop thinking about you."

"That's sweet and sappy, and exactly what I expected from my sheriff."

We stare into each other's eyes and I want to dive into his deep blue gaze.

"You and me, okay?" He says it like it's settled.

"Once you've settled things with Jarrod." He gets my stern sheriff voice.

Ben pouts adorably but he nods, knowing I mean it.

"And there's no patrol this morning. I'm tailing your ass to work, remember?

His eyes darken and I know he's thinking about me doing other things with his ass.

"You're a wicked man." I kiss him because I love all of his wickedness.

Ben snuggles against me. "And you're a good man, JD."

139

I want to tell him I'm his man, but I can't, not yet. Not until he's settled things with Jarrod.

* * *

I SHOULD HAVE KNOWN the day is going to go to the dogs when I hurry into the break room a few hours later, desperate for a coffee top up. Ben greets me as usual with coffee and a cannoli, but since then he's been stuck in his office with a steady stream of calls which he's fielding to the deputies. I contemplate making him a coffee, but think it will be a step too far for the office.

I rock back on my heels as I spot the newcomer.

"What the heck is this?"

Where once our old and cranky coffee (just like the sheriff) maker sat, a shiny new coffee machine gleams at me in the break room.

Of course Ben has to walk in and catch me scowling at it. He laughs at me as I glower.

"Need a lesson, Sheriff?"

"I need the old one. What happened to it?"

"It had a fight last night with Gloria and lost."

I grunt. Thanks to my clerk, I'm going to have to learn a new machine. It took me long enough to learn how to make coffee with the last coffee maker.

"I'll make you a coffee," Ben promises.

'I want to make my own one." I sound like a five-year-old having a temper tantrum. I feel like that small kid.

"I could show you if you like," he says as if uncertain how his offer will be received.

I smile at him. I really need to get over myself.

"Thanks. Okay, what do I have to do to get precious caffeine out of it?"

"You drink too much coffee."

"Let's not go there," I grouse.

No one, not even Ben, was going to come between me and my coffee.

He laughs at me and I smile at him. "It's easy. All you have to do is—"

"Sheriff?"

I look over to the door to see Gloria smiling uncertainly at me. "What is it, Gloria?"

"Mrs. Johnson is here and she wants to see you."

I glance at Ben, but he looks as confused as me. "Why does your mom need to see me. Is it about Sam?"

I thought we'd dealt with him last night. Was he in trouble again?

"I don't know. I haven't spoken to her since we saw her last night." His lips twitch. "I was kinda busy."

I see the curiosity all over Gloria's face. I am not going to satisfy that.

"Take her to my office," I say instead to her.

"Yes, Sheriff."

She vanishes and I look at Ben. "We'd better find out what your Mom wants."

We walk out of the break room and find Mrs. Johnson right there. Usually the woman is sweet and full of apologies as she tries to handle her wayward youngest son. But now she is furious, her eyes flashing, and it's all aimed at me. I take a step back, not sure what I've done to inspire such fury.

"Momma, what are you doing here?" Ben asks.

"Jarrod told me what was going on and I didn't believe him."

I feel Ben stiffen beside me.

"Jarrod told you what exactly?"

I'm suddenly aware everyone staring our way in the open office. "Why don't we have this discussion in my office."

She shakes her head and her curls, so like her son's, bounce around her face. She pushes them away impatiently.

"We talk here. You've been leading my son astray."

My cheeks heat. "Mrs. Johnson—"

But she didn't let me speak.

"He's a married man and you're his boss. It's a misuse of power. You should be sacked."

"Momma," Ben barks.

And for the first time she looks at him. "Jarrod told me and I didn't believe him until I saw your car outside his house. You're married."

Ben is crimson with embarrassment but also anger. "Jarrod is only my husband because he didn't sign the divorce papers. You know that."

"In the eyes of God—"

"God? You know how I feel about religion. But if we're talking about God, does it mention motorcycle clubs in the Bible? Does God mention the way I was abused by Jarrod? Is that okay in God's eyes?"

By now Mrs. Johnson is as red as her son was. "Don't be rude to me."

But Ben is too furious to back down. "You're being disrespectful to the Sheriff and blind if you think Jarrod treated me like a husband should."

It's only going to go south from here. I need to intervene before they both say something they can't walk back.

"Mrs. Johnson, let's go into my office. This is a personal discussion."

She turns on me and I take a step back.

"I thought you were a decent man. A pillar of our community. Instead, you're preying on young men."

I want to groan. This is exactly why I didn't get involved with Ben.

"He is a decent man," Ben almost yells. 'Unlike Jarrod.

142

He. Abused. Me. Physically and mentally. Do you want me to tell you what he did to me? I can show you the scars.

Mrs. Johnson covers her mouth. "Ben—"

"And I'm the one who made the first move on JD. Me. Not him."

Everyone in the office is fixed on us. For some reason Gloria looks satisfied. I wonder if she approves of Mrs. Johnson reaming me out. Then I catch her gaze and she gives me an almost fond smile. She likes that Ben is declaring his feelings for me.

"He should have said no," Mrs. Johnson spits. "It's not right."

She is right. I should have no, no matter how much I want this sweet man with a heart of sunshine in my life.

"Mrs. Johnson—"

"You stay away from my son. He's a married man."

I'm ready to lose it a little at this point. She doesn't seem to care about the abuse. Ben deserves so much better than Jarrod. He deserves better than me. But I want to give him the world.

"Momma, I'm taking you home," Ben says, and I can tell he's almost in tears.

She ignores her son and skewers me with a scowl. I could take lessons from her. "I trust I make myself clear."

"I think you should leave now, Mrs. Johnson." I'm proud of my even tone.

She opens her mouth, but Ben tugs her away.

"Now, Mom, before he arrests you and fires me."

I blink because that's the last thing on my mind but the threat seems to work and she allows Ben to hustle her out of the office.

In the silence that follows, I don't know what to do, but when I turn, all my co-workers are focused on their jobs,

143

except Gloria. She stares at me with a pity that makes me want to shrivel up.

"Coffee, Sheriff Morgan?" she asks. "Ben's shown me how to work the new machine."

"Thanks. That'd be good." I stalk into my office and shut the door. And I'm ready to add a whiskey chaser.

Five minutes later there's a soft tap at the door and she comes in with a large cup of coffee and a plate with a cannoli.

I'm waiting for her to say something, but Gloria places them on the table and leaves me alone to dwell in my misery.

The coffee has too much creamer and not enough sugar, but I'm grateful for her kindness. I push the pastry to one side. It reminds me too much of Ben.

He returns to work after taking his mother home and hides in the dispatch office. Gloria takes care of him too. It's a relief not to see him to be honest. I don't think I could cope trying to hide my feelings right now. The one thing I do know is I can't continue to work with Ben and pretend that I don't want him. I'm not that good an actor.

I place a call to Sheriff Bob in the next county. I was going to call him and now is the right time.

"JD, it's a surprise to hear from you," he booms.

I take a deep breath. "Bob, I need your help."

"It's got to be bad if you pick up the phone to me."

"It is. And I launch into my piles of woes, starting with Eric Kent.

None of my co-workers say anything to me beyond a cheery goodnight as I head for the door at the end of the day. They seem determined to ignore the elephant in the room. I grunt my goodbyes and scowl as I leave the office.

I falter as I see Ben by my car. He looks terrified and determined at the same time. I want to take him in my arms and hold him, tell him that he is mine forever. Instead I shove my hands in my pockets and keep him at a distance. I need to be stronger than him, show him his mom was right.

"We need to talk," he says.

"I don't think now's the right time," I say, but Ben shakes his head and plows on.

"Momma, she didn't know about me and you. She's just shocked, is all. She'll get used to the idea."

I sigh. "There isn't a me and you, Ben. She was right about one thing. I'm too old for you. We need to remember that. I'm going home."

To forget this day ever happened and try to find the remains of my dignity.

"You promised to stay by my side."

"I did. That was before I knew you had a husband."

I hate using Jarrod as an excuse, but Ben deserves better than me. His momma knows best. Ben is young enough to move on and find a lovely man his own age. I can just nurse my heartache from a distance.

He looks as if he wants to argue, but for once my scowl works and he steps back. I resolutely ignore the fact he stares after me as I drive away.

I open my front door and gratefully stumble through, needing to shut out the world. I head for the refrigerator and pull out a beer. I pop the cap, down the bottle in one and throw it in the trash, then collapse on the sofa and close my eyes.

"There's no fool like an old fool, JD," I say into the silence of the room. "You've gotta remember that."

18

COLLIER'S CREEK
small town romance

BEN

I spend an hour sitting in my car outside my house, wondering what to do. Do I go talk to JD? Will he even open the door to me? I've no idea. He must be furious after that showdown with my momma. He was so cold when he left. I hoped he would talk to me but he just drove away. In the end I reverse out of my drive and head to JD's. I have to try.

I hear footsteps approach the door, then a pause, he must be looking through the peephole.

"Please open the door." Do I call him sheriff or JD?

The door opens and JD regards me. I wince at his sad and tired expression. He's never looked like that before when he talks to me. I try again with the conversation I wanted to have earlier.

"I'm so sorry, I really am. I had no idea Momma was gonna confront you like that."

The pain in his eyes hurts me so much. "It's no more than

I deserve. She's right. I'm too old for you."

"That's not true."

"I'm older than your Momma."

"You're younger than her." He raises an eyebrow and I blush on Momma's behalf. "She shaves a few years off her age now she's trying to date."

His lips twitch and I know he's holding back what he wants to say, but my sheriff is a gentleman and he would never be rude about her to my face.

"Please can I come in?" I beg.

He hesitates, but then he steps back. I push past him into the dim hall, wait until he's shut the door, then I step right into his space and grab his collar. I can smell beer on his breath. JD tries to step back but I won't let him. I'm not sure where the sudden bravery comes from, but I need him to know that he's the one that I want.

"It's only you, JD. It's only ever been you. I've wanted you since I was fourteen and just discovered I was gay." I blushed furiously at my confession.

"You knew you were gay at fourteen?"

I frown at him. He seems to be missing the point. "Which bit of I've wanted you forever did you miss?"

"I'm trying to get over the skeevy feeling of being lusted after by a teenager when I was in my thirties."

I deflate. "Oh, right." He has a point. "But you were—are—really hot."

There's no way I'm ever going to confess it was much much earlier than fourteen. He'd never be able to handle that. And it was my first crush. We all had them. My friends lusted after pop singers and movie stars. Mine was the hot deputy sheriff closer to home. I never thought I'd be able to act on it almost eight years later.

"Why did you go away?"

"I wanted to get out of Collier's Creek. You know that." I

147

pluck up my courage to ask a question I've wanted to know forever. "When did you first notice me?"

He hesitates. "You were legal. That's all I'm going to say. And I was never going near you."

I kiss his cheek. "You know what? It doesn't matter."

I see the relief in his expression and I decide to let sleeping crushes lie.

"Take me to bed," I beg.

"What about Jarrod?"

"I've filed for divorce. He can't ignore it this time."

He gathers me in close for a hug that's so tender I want to cry.

"You get divorced from him before we make any big announcements, okay?"

I want to point out that my momma killed any idea of secrecy with her screaming fit in the middle of our office. Besides which, according to the oracle that is Gloria, the whole of Collier's Creek know how we feel about each other.

"How did it take this long?" I mutter.

"We had to be ready," he rumbles above me, "and I take a long time to decide anything. You know what I'm like."

I know that. It took him long enough to be able to accept morning cannolis. He never realized I was only buying them for him, not the whole office. I'm a lowly dispatcher. I don't get paid that much.

I yawn against his shoulder, the stress of the day catching up with me.

JD holds me tight "Tired?

"Exhausted. Take me to bed."

"I was gonna suggest I offer you a ride home."

I hear the amusement in his voice.

"No, I want to sleep with you naked. I'm too tired for any fun stuff but I want to sleep resting my head against your chest and listening to your heart beat."

There was a long pause, then, "I think we can do that. If you're sure."

"I'm sure."

JD leads me to his bedroom. It's a lot tidier than mine and the bed is made.

"You might have an issue with how untidy I am," I say.

His lips quirk up. "Like your desk?"

I bite my bottom lip. "You'd do that?"

"If it stops me breaking a leg."

One of the few times JD reprimanded me was for the mess around my desk. I used eat candy and chips and throw the wrappers around the desk. He pointed out in no uncertain terms the cleaners weren't my maids. He presented me with a trash can and I was to use it. I was mortified but I never made a mess like that again.

"I'll clean up when you're with me," I promise.

"I'll help you." JD kisses my forehead. "I'm going to undress you now."

And he undresses me, not like it's foreplay, but like I'm tired and he wants to help me, and encourage me into bed. When he tucks me in I really do feel like a small boy.

"Aren't you coming to bed?"

The idea had been both of us together, not me in a strange bed by myself.

"I'm gonna make sure everything is locked up. Then I'll come to bed. Five minutes, tops."

I huff a little and he's grinning as he walks out of the bedroom. I smile too but I also breathe a sigh of relief because I hadn't been sure he'd let me in the house. He was really upset when he left. At some point I'm gonna have to have a long conversation with my momma about the way she treated JD. No one hurts my sheriff. I won't let them.

Which reminds me to set my alarm so I'll be up for the early shift for work.

Four minutes and thirty seconds later he slides into bed, and we roll together, skin to skin. I rest my head on his chest and hear the satisfying thump of his heart under my ear. It's the best sound in the world.

* * *

I DON'T WANT to leave JD sleeping peacefully, but I'm doing the early shift and he doesn't have to go in until later. I leave him with a kiss on his stubbly cheek and a whispered "I love you."

I don't know if he heard it because he doesn't seem to wake up but from the smile that curves his lips I think it permeates his dreams.

I drive to my place to shower and change. I've only got fifteen minutes so I jog up the stoop to the front door. As I open the front door, something shoves me from behind. I stumble forward, trying to catch my balance, only for someone to grab my hair and yank me painfully backward against him. Before I have time to react, I recognize the stale tobacco smell.

"Time to say goodbye, Ben."

"You're leaving?"

Hope makes my heart skip a beat, only to dash it in the next second.

"*We're* leaving this shithole town now." Jarrod spits out each word like it offends him.

Collier's Creek is my home. His insult plenty offends me.

"I can't leave," I protest. "I'm supposed to be at work in ten minutes."

"You resigned," he says with a smug grin. "I called them and told them you weren't coming back."

I look at him in horror. "You didn't. You had no right!"

He sneers at me. "You're married to me. You don't get a

choice. The old man was really upset that you're not coming back."

I ignore his crack about the old man. Jarrod is just trying to wind me up. He couldn't have spoken to JD as I left him sleeping ten minutes ago.

"This is 2023, not 1953. Even if we were together, you don't get to make decisions for me."

"Understand one thing, sweetheart."

The endearment grinds across my heart. Only JD has the right to call me sweetheart.

Jarrod continues, thankfully unaware of my thoughts. "You're my husband, which makes you my property, and I tell you what you can do."

I shake my head. "No. This is my home and I'm going to stay here."

"You hate Collier's Creek. You always said so."

"That was then. But my mom and brother are here, my job is here, and I'm good at what I do."

His sneer turns nasty. "That include the old guy?"

My heart stops. "I don't know what you mean."

"I think you do. The old man. The sheriff. You do him too? I see the way he looks at you. I caught you in his arms. Do you have to dick him as part of the job? He can't get it up, hmm?"

I never hated him as much as I did in that moment. "I'm a dispatcher, not a whore. You're the one who wanted to whore me out. And Sheriff Morgan isn't old."

From his flat chuckle I probably give myself away the second I mention JD's name.

"Whatever you say, sweetheart."

It's the way he drawls sweetheart for the second time that gives me the clue. I stare at him. "You heard him call me that. You've never called me sweetheart before."

Jarrod's lip curled. "Clever boy. It's disgusting. You

throwing yourself at an old man. It'd been a shame if that information gets into the wrong hands."

Icy tendrils clutch at my heart. "What do you mean by that?" I demand.

He leans forward and grabs my chin, his fingers digging painfully into my neck. I stay still, afraid he's going to hurt me more. It wouldn't be the first time.

"Let's do a deal, sweetheart. You come with me and I don't tell the town that their old sheriff has been sticking his dick in another man's property."

"I'm not your property."

'As far as the club is concerned, you are, and as far as the town is concerned, you're married and I know these small towns. They hate affairs."

I say nothing, especially the fact that they probably all know by now. Jarrod smirks as if I've agreed with him.

"We're gonna go and your sheriff gets to live."

I pull back in horror. "What the hell, Jarrod?"

"He's touched what's mine. As far as the club is concerned he gets a bullet in the back of the head."

"I'll go with you," I say shakily. "Just leave him alone."

Jarrod regards me for a long while. "Deal."

I hope JD forgives me for walking out on him but I can't risk his life.

"I need to pack my gear."

Jarrod shakes his head and hooks his hand around my bicep, again gripping me so painfully I couldn't pull away. I was so conscious of the gentle way JD handled me compared to Jarrod. "You're not taking anything ."

"But I'll need clothes."

"No. You can wear what I find for you at the clubhouse. Give me your phone."

I stare at him. "No."

He cocks his fingers, as if aiming a gun.

"Fuck you."

I stagger back at the open-handed slap across the face.

"Give me your phone."

I hand it over and without even looking at it, he drops it and stamps on it, shattering the screen. I blink back the tears. The phone was one of the first things I bought when I returned to Collier's Creek.

"Never mind, sweetheart. You won't need a phone where you're going."

I shiver. It sounds as if he wants to put me in the ground.

He drags me out of the house. Suddenly my front yard is full of motorcycles. I didn't see them as I drove up so I've no idea where they've been hiding.

"About time," Ink snarls. I hadn't seen him in town before. He must have been with Jarrod while the others checked me out. He was covered in tattoos from head to toe. "Thought you'd decided to make nice with the ball and chain."

I glare at him and they hoot with laughter. I can see the chains wrapping around me with every second.

"Let's get out of here," Jarrod snarled.

Within seconds we're riding through Collier's Creek. I scan the Main Street, hoping to find anyone who knows me, but the sidewalks are empty. No one will see me leave town.

The club turn onto the highway and Jarrod stops abruptly.

"What the fuck," Jarrod spits.

I look up for the first time and see…police cruisers in the middle of the road, and Aimee and Ted and Brad in front of them. Behind them are tractors blocking the road

What are they doing here? Where is JD?

Jarrod is furious, anger radiating through him. "What's the hell's going on?"

But I know. For the first time since Jarrod rolled into

153

town, I have hope. My town has my back. Now where is my sheriff?

19

JD

The sound of my cell phone wakes me up, but before I can fumble for it on the nightstand, it stops. I'm about to roll over and go back to sleep when it starts again.

"Sake," I bark and jam the phone against my ear. "Morgan."

"Sheriff?"

"Gloria, is everything okay?" I never heard that particular note in her voice before. She sounded on the verge of tears.

"Ben's been kidnapped."

I sat bolt upright, ignoring the painful twinge in my lower back. My heart stopped.

No, not my Ben.

"What?"

"He's been kidnapped. His husband called in and said Ben wasn't coming back. Then old Mrs. Robinson saw him being forced onto a motorcycle."

Anger roiled through me. I shoved the phone on speaker and threw on my uniform. "When?"

"About five minutes ago. She called 911 immediately. I was covering for Tom."

Dammit, they'd be out of town before I reached my car.

"Deputy Warren is following them and Deputy Murphy is waiting the other side of town. He'll delay them until you get there. I alerted them when Mr. Stoltz called here."

"Good thinking, Gloria."

I praised her actions. It was quick thinking. But we wouldn't be able to hold them for long.

"I'm on my way," I promise her, grabbing my badge and wallet, and holstering my service weapon.

"The guys from the farm have blocked the highway with tractors but I don't think it'll stop them."

I groan, not wanting civilians involved. I was going to spend weeks soothing the state troopers' ruffled feathers.

"They promise not to start a fight."

I grunt. I know these guys. They'd start a ruckus over an extra hash brown.

"Let me know when we have them blocked."

"Yessir."

I slam on the lights and sirens and scream through Collier's Creek. I just pray no one is foolish enough to get in my way.

I arrive to a standoff of red and blue flashing lights and deputies staring at the motorcycles revving their engines. Farm equipment block the road and men from Collier's Creek stand nearby, not interfering but just there.

I seek out Ben. He's still on the back of Jarrod's Hog. Jarrod has him by a firm grip, not letting him go.

Murphy nods at me. "Sheriff."

I nod back, understanding they were all waiting for me.

"Morgan." Jarrod snarls, immediately putting me on edge.

"Sheriff," I corrected.

"What do you want, Sheriff?" He doesn't try to hide the sarcasm in his tone.

I nod at Ben, trying to gauge his expression.

"I think you're leaving with someone who doesn't want to leave town."

Have I made a huge mistake? Ben's huge eyes are on me. Not him. His whole focus is on me. And he seems to be pleading with me. I'm not sure what he's asking for. Does he want me to let him go?

"He came willingly."

"We'll see," I say neutrally. I don't want to provoke a fight. Jarrod is clearly trigger-happy. I did my research. It turns out Jarrod is new to the presidency. He took over when the last guy died, of natural causes from every thing I read. Jarrod was his second and he's more volatile. I wonder how long he'll last.

"He stays with me," Jarrod snarls. "He's mine."

I give him a cool look. "Ben makes his own choices. He's an adult. No one makes a decision for him. Not you. Not me. Ben decides."

"He's *my* husband."

I'm aware of my deputies moving around the scene as the townsfolk stay in the background, calm, not moving an inch. Aimee and Warren are handling the traffic. I hear heated conversations and the sound of vehicles pulling away. Tim and Brad are between the other bikers and Jarrod. They seem relaxed enough and I know the MC well enough to know a small-town conflict is not their beef. Collier's Creek is below their pay grade. However, in their mind they owned their women. Was Ben any different?

The tension makes my skin crawl, if worry were bugs, but my attention is trained on Jarrod and Ben. If Jarrod erupts then Ben could get hurt. I'd die before letting Ben be injured or worse.

"Ben, come over here." I hold out my hand. "We'll talk, then you can decide."

He hesitates, and my heart sinks. I think again, have I really just made a huge mistake and potentially put the town in danger?

Jarrod spat, aiming toward my boots. "He doesn't want to go. Now get out of our way."

But Ben slides off the Hog, evading Jarrod's attempt to stop him, and hurries over to me.

"Watch him," I say to Murphy, gesturing at Jarrod.

Murphy nods and fixes his cold regard on him. He's a big guy, easily makes two of me. I hope he gives Jarrod something to think about. On the other hand, we've just cornered Jarrod. Who knows how he's going to react?

But that's for my deputies to handle. I have to find out what Ben really wants.

I gently move Ben to put myself between him and Jarrod. I don't like turning my back on Jarrod, but I'm going to shield my boy.

"Sheriff, you've got to let me go," Ben starts.

"Are you all right?" I ask gently, ignoring his words.

Ben stares at me with wide eyes. He's terrified, I can see that. It doesn't look as if he's slept in days, dark marks like bruising under his eyes, yet he slept in my arms. If I find out Jarrod has assaulted him, all bets are off.

"Ben, do you want to go with Jarrod?"

His hands shake and he shoves them under his armpits, trying to hide his trembling. I want to take him in my arms and soothe him.

"Ben?"

"No," he says in low voice. "I don't want to go, but I've got no choice. If I don't go, he says he'll hurt…"

He trails off and I narrow my eyes.

"Who does he say he'll hurt?"

Ben presses his lips together.

"If he's threatening someone, I need to know. Who is Jarrod threatening to hurt?"

"You," Ben mutters. "He says he's going to hurt you and I can't have that."

I let out a breath. I'm not surprised. I knew Jarrod would go for the jugular.

"He's not going to touch me," I assure him. I step closer into Ben's space and he trembles. "He's just trying to scare you."

"He succeeded," Ben retorts, "but you don't know him, JD. He'll shoot you as soon as look at you."

The use of my name rather than my title in public indicates how emotional he feels.

"Have you seen him do that?"

"No, but he used to talk about it all the time."

Some men were like that. All mouth, but no action. The ones I was more frightened of were the guys who didn't mouth off but waited in a quiet corner one night and shot you in the back of the head. I wasn't sure about Jarrod. I'd checked him out. He'd hurt plenty of men but usually with his fists.

But that isn't important right now.

"Ben, don't leave because you're frightened about me. I can handle myself. Do you want to go with him?" I take the leap off the cliff. "Or do you want to stay in Collier's Creek, with me?"

His eyes go so wide it's almost comical. "With you?"

I nod, hoping I've not made a total idiot of myself.

"You want me?" His voice is so small I want to stride over to Jarrod and punch him in the face for doing a number on my man's self-esteem. Because Ben is all mine.

"I want you so much." I give him a tender smile. "But you need to stay here in Collier's Creek so I can show you."

"You mean it? You're not just saying that?"

"You know I'm not. You and me, we're made for each other. I was going to tell you when Jarrod rolled into town."

"I'm frightened," he admits.

"Of Jarrod?" Ben shakes his head and I furrow my brow. "Of me?"

Ben had never shown any fear around me. He laughed and joked, treated me with a gentle respect I'd come to know and love. I thought he had feelings for me. Had I gotten it all wrong?

"I'm frightened you'll think...less of me because of this."

"If we were on our own, I'd show you exactly what I think of you," I murmur. "But as we're surrounded by our co-workers and friends, I'll keep it PG. Leave him and be with me forever."

Ben gives me the smallest of nods. I take his hand as the knot around my heart eases for the first time since Ben told me Jarrod was his husband.

"Where's all your gear?" I ask.

"He didn't let me take anything."

Anger flares at Jarrod treating him like property. I bite back the angry words and instead look over my shoulder.

"Deputy Sheriff Murphy, escort Stoltz and the club out of town. Ensure they don't come back. Ben is staying here."

"You'll regret it, Morgan," Jarrod bellowed.

I turn to face him, making sure Ben is behind me. "Sheriff Morgan, and we've all heard your threat to me. Leave now before I arrest of all you."

"Let's go, Ace," one of his men mutters. "He's just one whore. He's not worth it."

I turn on him and so does Jarrod, and for one

infinitesimal moment, I thaw toward Jarrod, until he gives a scornful laugh.

'You're right. You like sloppy seconds, *Sheriff*? He's all yours."

"I knew that already," I say and give him a lazy wave. "He always was."

I hear Ben choke but my focus is on Stoltz.

Jarrod is furious, but he's lost. There's nothing he can do. He guns the Hog. The club rumble down the road, escorted by my deputies.

I tug Ben into my arms and make sure the last thing Jarrod sees in his mirror is me kissing his soon-to-be-very-ex-husband.

Ben is shocked, I can tell. It takes him a few seconds to react, but then his arms are around my neck and he's kissing me back just as enthusiastically.

A cough breaks into our moment.

"They're gone. If you can put it each other down..." Aimee says.

So maybe it had gotten past a PG rating.

I raised my head and looked at my deputy. "We should contact the state troopers."

She rolls her eyes. "Already done."

I grin at her and sling an arm around Ben's shoulders. I think that shocks her more than the kiss.

"Ben needs a ride home," I say.

Aimee nods. "I'll do it. I can take his statement at the same time."

Ben swallows. "Do I still have a job?"

"That's up to you," I say, "but for now go home and rest. You're exhausted."

"But—"

"Home. Sleep," I order.

Aimee leads him away. Ben looks over his shoulder, but

he goes obediently. I turn to my deputies and the townsfolk staring at me.

"Are we gonna have a problem?"

I deliberately catch each of their gazes. I want to know now before this becomes public knowledge.

Will shrugs his shoulders. "It's about time you two quit mooning over each other."

"You knew?"

I receive a round of eye-rolling that lets me know, yes, they knew, and could I be more stupid?

"Well." I cough, doing my best not to go crimson. "Thank you for your help."

I shake everyone's hand, including my deputies.

"Just doing our job," one of them mutters.

"I know, but thanks, I appreciate it."

"You still gonna get shit from us all," he points out.

"I know that too," I say cheerfully.

He gives me a strange look. "That's freaky, you know?"

I furrow my brow. "What is?"

"You smiling. It's not right."

I scowl at him and he visibly relaxes. What the heck?

"That's the sheriff I know and love."

Then he walks off, leaving me staring at him.

"You know they're not gonna let you live this down, don't you?"

I turn to Murphy. "Have you got a problem with me?"

He shrugs. "I could do without seeing you kissing every five seconds."

"It was once."

"That's enough for a lifetime," he assures me. "My wife doesn't like it if I watch PDA."

I couldn't help my laugh. "I know the books your wife reads. She's lying to you."

"I know that. I just let her think she doesn't. It's what couples do."

And with that he knocks the wind out of my sails. A couple. We're a couple now. That's if Ben wants to be.

He eyes me shrewdly. "Make your report, Sheriff, then go talk to Ben."

"Do you want to become my Undersheriff?" I ask.

"Is that a formal offer?"

"It's an acting position until I get all the red tape sorted out."

"I accept."

"You know we've still got trash to deal with?"

"I heard," he says grimly.

"That's for later and it's gonna take time."

Eric Kent isn't going anywhere for a while. Sheriff Bob and I agreed we need to discover how far the rot goes. Does it stop with Kent or are others involved?

"First let's get rid of this trash," I say.

"And Ben?"

"I'm gonna have all the deputies report to you."

Murphy narrows his eyes. "You want to make Ben a deputy."

"I do," I admit. "But he needs training and he can't work for me directly."

"You both understand that he works for me and he can't use you to get what he wants."

I raise an eyebrow. "Has he ever done that?"

"No," he acknowledges. "But he's never been yours before."

"We tie this down in writing. If it doesn't work then I'll leave." I grimace. "After today I might not be the sheriff for much longer."

"People might surprise you," Murphy says.

I didn't say that very few people surprised me. I'm a good judge of character and I know who liked me and who didn't, and I know who'd have an issue with a gay sheriff and who wouldn't.

I walk back to my vehicle and slide behind the wheel with a sigh of relief. He's staying. Ben's staying and he wants to be with me. I let go of the fear that Ben would leave me for the guy on the Harley and immediately a new set of concerns took its place.

I speak to myself in the rearview mirror. "Just one night, JD. Quit panicking for just one night and think about Ben. He's the only person you have to worry about."

I stare at myself for a long moment.

"What if he changes his mind?"

20

BEN

*T*he day stretches on endlessly and I still don't see the one person I want to talk to. I curl up under a fleece blanket and shiver. I know I'm safe now, but I can't quite get my head around it.

Momma and Sam turn up on my doorstep. She cries over me and apologizes for her part in the whole saga. She hadn't realized Jarrod wanted to kidnap me and make me his…we dance around the word. She also talks about JD, she's working on her feelings about that. One thing at a time.

Sam is the biggest surprise of all. As Momma gets in the car, he turns to me.

"I hated you for dropping out of college. I didn't realize…" He trails off.

I nod because not telling my family was my mistake, not his. In his eyes I took his dream and threw it away.

"We'll talk, soon, yeah? Maybe we'll find a way of both of us getting what we want." Whatever that is.

He nods too, not looking convinced, then he jogs to the car.

I watch them drive away, wishing JD was here. I need someone to lean on.

Gloria comes around after her shift to give the gossip. Normally I'd shush her, okay, maybe that's a lie. But today I want all the information.

"Mom made bear claws for you." She handed me a Tupperware box which had to have come from the 1980s.

"That's kind of her," I said, putting it next to me. I hadn't felt like eating all day. I'm still so scared.

"She made some for the sheriff too."

I squint at her. "Really?"

Gloria beams at me. "I love my mom."

So did I.

"Sheriff Morgan's your hero," Gloria says gleefully. "I thought he was gonna haul all of them back here."

I shiver again. "I went willingly. There's nothing to arrest them for."

She rolls her eyes. "There's willing and *willing*."

I went because I was afraid for JD and my family. But they couldn't arrest Jarrod for that.

"Anyway, I think you're the hero," I say sincerely. "You mobilized the cavalry."

Gloria beams at me. "Yeah, I did. You would have done it for me."

"Yeah, I would. But thank you."

I lean forward and kiss her cheek.

Gloria bites her bottom lip, then she says, "The sheriff spoke to all of us. He said what Jarrod tried to do was horrible. He thanked us all."

"That's kind of him."

She nods, then gives me a mischievous grin. "He was

amazing. Not grumpy at all, even though I parked in his space again. He said I was distracted."

I roll my eyes and she giggles.

I'm pleased to see Gloria, she's a good friend even if she does drive me crazy sometimes. Still I'm glad when she's gone. I need time to think without anyone here. To process what happened today.

The town saved me. They came out for me and the sheriff. When I saw JD arrive and everyone else in the middle of the highway, I wanted to laugh and scream and cry. Jarrod wouldn't understand.

"They were there for *me*," I say into the silence of the room.

He was so tied up with the MC it never occurred to him that there were other connections, other families.

I've always lived in Collier's Creek until I went to college. I thought going to school would give me the chance to escape. Now I know I belong here. But who to?

I shiver under the blanket. I still can't believe Jarrod is out of my life. I won't believe it until it's all wrapped up legally. JD's lawyer friend called me and promised to get all the paperwork underway and served as soon as possible. He didn't actually do anything and I agreed to go with him. There's nothing the cops can arrest him for. But we'll get the divorce sorted and that will be the end of it. He'll be gone and I'll be free.

I sigh as the doorbell crackles into life. So much for having time to process. As I fling open the door, I think maybe that wasn't the most sensible thing to do after nearly being kidnapped.

"You should have asked who it was," JD grumbled. "Do you want to be kidnapped again?"

I just stare at him. "You."

JD blinks. "Me?"

"Why didn't you come sooner?"

"I waited because I knew you'd have your mom, family, and friends."

JD didn't admit he was avoiding Momma but I understood.

"I only wanted you," I say. "You saved me."

"It wasn't just me." He stares down at his hands. "I'd go to the ends of the earth for you."

"For me?"

"Of course you. You know I would," he groused. "Don't be stupid. You know I love you."

And I did know that because he showed it in every look and every gesture, even when he thought I didn't notice. I always noticed.

"JD." My voice cracks just a little.

"Yes?"

"I want you to take me to bed and make me forget all about today."

"Are you…"

"If you're about to ask if I'm sure, yes I'm fucking sure."

I tugged him inside the house and shut the door on the outside world. There were somethings the neighbours didn't need to see, like the sheriff kissing his dispatcher.

"You know Mrs. Robinson will be on the phone to your momma," JD says. "She saw me pull up in your drive."

"I don't care."

"Your momma does," JD says ruefully. "She thinks I'm too old for you."

"I don't care."

"But—"

I fix him with a level stare. "JD, after today, you're fucking golden with my family and the town. You could tap-dance naked around the square and they'd say you're just letting off steam. You saved me. Don't you get that?

You saved me. As for the rest of the town, their sheriff is a hero."

By now JD is an interesting shade of red. I chuckle and stroke his cheek, feeling the rasp of his bristles under my palm. "Nothing matters except I love you."

I expect a protest, another comment about being too old for me, but JD steps into my space, tilts my chin, and kisses me. I melt against him, open my mouth to his and let our tongues dance together. This is the way we should be talking. Words get in the way of communication.

I gasp as he picks me up and carries me to my bedroom. "You're so strong."

Geez, I sound like the heroine in a Regency romance, and from the way JD snorts, he thinks so too. I will *never* admit to reading my momma's books. Ever. Not even on pain of death.

Instead I wrap my arms around his neck and snuggle into him. I want to be fucked but snuggling is good too.

For once I don't care about the state of my bedroom and JD doesn't seem to notice as he drops me on the unmade bed, and climbs on top of me to reclaim my mouth.

His kisses are sweet and drugging, not domineering and cruel like Jarrod's were. I push away the thought of my ex-husband. He doesn't deserve any space in our bed.

But JD raises his head. "What's wrong?"

"Nothing," I lie.

"I felt you shiver. Tell me. Did I hurt you?" He looks concerned and I hasten to reassure him.

"I love your kisses. I'm sorry, I thought about Jarrod. He hurt me when he kissed me."

I expect JD to get all angry, but instead he holds me close and brushes his mouth across mine.

"It's okay. It's going to take time to stop thinking about him. If I do anything to hurt or scare you, just let me know."

I cup his jaw. "You would never scare me. You don't have it in you."

To my surprise he grins.

"You know I'm the sheriff, right? I'm supposed to be big and scary."

I want to point out he's laying on top of me, his hard dick pushing into my hip, his lips glistening and puffy, his eyes soft and kind. Big and scary wasn't cutting it.

"You're not scary to the people that matter."

"Like you?"

"Like me," he agrees.

JD smooths the back of his finger across my cheekbone. My toes curl and I let out a moan I'm not proud of.

I reach up for another kiss and any discussions of soon-to-be-ex-husbands or scary sheriffs fade away. The only thing that matters is the two of us in this bed.

* * *

I HAVE my head on JD's belly, my fingers lightly tugging at the short hairs as I lay there, barely able to move. We had just finished what felt like a marathon of lovemaking, and now I 'm completely boneless. His fingers begin to make lazy circles on my back, slowly calming my racing heart. The sweat and pungent musk of our lovemaking lingers in the air, an amber reminder of the hours we have just spent exploring each other's bodies.

I let out a heavy sigh, feeling utterly exhausted. All the adrenaline that had been coursing through my veins has crashed and burned, draining me of all my energy and leaving me limp and spent. Yet I feel content, satisfied, and incredibly peaceful—like I'm exactly where I'm meant to be. JD's fingers continue to lazily trail up and down my back, tracing patterns that lull me into a calm, almost trance-like state.

I close my eyes, allowing myself to just drift away and savor the moment. This is bliss, I think, contentment like I've never experienced before. I've never felt so wanted and loved by anyone. I don't want to move, ever.

"Ben?"

It's the first word either of us has spoken in ages and I'm almost asleep.

"Hmmm?" I say it to his belly. I'm too tired to raise my head.

"Do you still want to leave Collier's Creek?"

At that, I do raise my head to look at him. I wasn't expecting life-changing discussions after a marathon love-making session. This isn't a conversation I can have playing with his body hair.

"I don't know," I admit. "I've been too busy to think about it. You know I always wanted to leave here."

His eyes are hooded and I can't read his expression. "Is that why you were willing to leave with Stoltz?"

"Hell no. I wouldn't have been living my life with him. He wanted to imprison me."

"But your dreams are bigger than Collier's Creek."

"I wanted to be a deputy. You know that."

"I do. You wanted to become a deputy sheriff but away from here. Starting somewhere new."

His voice is bland and I can't decide if he's asking me or telling me.

"It is my dream."

Now I'm not so sure that's still true. It *was* my dream, but that would mean moving away from JD and I'm sure how I feel about that. It's not going to happen.

"But you came home."

"I wanted to get away from Jarrod and Sam was spinning

off the rails. Momma needed me. I had nowhere else to go." I furrow my brow. "Why are you asking me this?"

My lazy sex-haze vanishes in a cloud of fear and confusion as I stare at JD. His eyes and mouth are pinched and he seems to be searching for the right words. Tension coils in my gut. Is he asking me to leave? Would that make life easier for him?

"I'm going to need a new deputy sheriff soon." Before I can speak he puts a finger over my lips. "Look, I can't talk to you about what's happening, but there will be a vacancy in the future, if you want it."

I understand. This is about Eric Kent, but he can't tell me. I guess we'll have many conversations like this if we stay together.

"Me?" I ask the question, just to be sure.

"I'm sure we've had this conversation," he rumbles. "Yes, you."

"Are you sure?"

"I can't think of anyone I want more than you by my side."

I bury my face in JD's belly, overwhelmed by his admission.

"If you prefer, I could ask around for positions in other counties. You don't have to work here."

"No. I mean, yes, I want to apply for the deputy's job. Won't it be awkward, you being my boss?"

"I'm your boss now," JD points out.

"But you weren't my lover before."

"True. But I'm promoting Ray Murphy to be my undersheriff. He'll be your direct manager."

I smile at him. "He's a good choice."

And I'm much happier at the thought of not working directly for JD. I had been thinking of finding another job, but he didn't need to know that.

"I thought so." JD grimaces. "It's been pointed out I spend

too much time in the field and not enough behind my desk. I need someone to take over from me in the field."

"You talked to Sheriff Bob."

"I did," he says sourly.

I press a kiss against his nipple. I know it's a sacrifice for him to give up the day-to-day police work he loves.

He hisses and fidgets underneath me. I lick his nipple to see what reaction I get. It's…interesting. JD really likes me playing with his nipples.

"Stop," he orders, his voice hoarse. "I want to finish this conversation before we get back to playtime."

I pout, but I wait to see what he's got to say.

"We need someone to train as an EMT later on. I'm going to do that first and then I want you to train. No one else in the office is interested."

"Really." I beam at him. "Yes, when can I start?"

JD chuckles. "One thing at a time. As soon as you're back in the office, we'll fill out the forms. It's gonna take time to process the paperwork for you to become a deputy."

"I can wait." But not for long. "And we'll need a new dispatcher."

"We've got one."

"Who?"

"Gloria." He sees my wide-eyed stare. "She's ideal. She's friendly and keeps her head in the event of an emergency. She's just like you."

I'm not so sure about that, but people like and trust her. That's important. I think she'll be great in the role.

"Does she know?"

"I asked her and she said yes. You can train her."

She kept that quiet today and I thought she couldn't keep a secret.

I sigh and reach up for a kiss. I'm feeling all unsettled again. On the one hand, JD is offering me everything I've always wanted. Training to be a deputy and an EMT. On the other it means big changes and I'm not sure I'm ready for that.

"You don't seem happy," JD says.

Trust him to notice.

"Promise me if us working together is a problem we find a way to deal that doesn't mean we're over."

"Pinky swear," he says. Then he smiles. "Promise you won't get upset when I get grumpy with you."

"You never get grumpy with me," I point out.

He thought about it for a moment. "You're right. Why is that?"

"Because I just want to make your day better."

"Why?"

"Because I love you."

He smiles at me. "Say that again."

"Because I love you."

JD runs his hand down my back and I shiver. "I can never hear that enough."

"I wish I'd been brave enough to say it sooner."

"Likewise."

"But then I wouldn't have seen you ride the bad guy out of town."

His lips twitch. "You liked that?"

"It was very hot," I assure him and receive a smug grin.

Then his smile fades. "Not everyone is gonna be happy about our relationship."

I sit up, cross my legs, and place a finger across his mouth. "Fuck 'em."

JD leans back, taking my hand and kissing my fingers. His lips are soft and warm, and I feel my heart racing. "I love it when you talk dirty," he murmurs, his eyes glinting with mischief.

I laugh and push him away playfully. "Stop it, JD. We need to talk about this."

He sobers up, nodding. "I know. It's just... I've been thinking a lot about it lately."

"About what?"

"About us. About our future."

I feel a flutter of excitement in my stomach. "What do you mean?"

"I mean..." He takes a deep breath. "I mean, I want to be with you. Forever."

My heart swells with love and happiness. I can hardly believe what I'm hearing. "Are you asking me to marry you?"

He laughs, shaking his head. "Not yet. But soon. I promise. When everything is sorted out between us, I'll ask you to marry me. I love you and want to spend the rest of my life with you."

"I can't believe I'm going to get everything I've ever wanted." I'm overwhelmed and tears prickle the back of my eyes.

JD gathers me into his arms. "You're not the only one, I promise. I thought you were a distant dream and now I have you in my arms."

I lean back and look at him. "There's one thing we're missing though."

He looks confused. "What have I missed?"

"How do you feel about a dog?"

EPILOGUE

JD

I stalk into CC's, dripping hot, sweet coffee from head to foot, my scowl daring anyone to say a single word.

Will hands me the coffee in silence, but he doesn't try to hide his huge smirk.

I glower at him. "Thanks."

"I thought you'd get less clumsy now you—"

"He's always going to be a klutz," Ben interrupts fondly from behind me. "But it wasn't his fault this time. Barky caught him by surprise."

The mutt caught me in the groin, again. It took me five minutes to stand up.

"That dog's a menace," I mutter under my breath.

"Barkasaurus, did the nasty sheriff get in your way." Will bends down to croon to the dog who rushes past me to greet his favorite person, the one with the treats.

No one pays any attention to me fuming on one side. I'm

not a klutz, no matter what Ben says. Then I look down at my sticky uniform. He has a point, although this time it isn't me daydreaming about what I'm going to do to Ben tonight, and everything to do with Barky yapping, and leaping at me at the wrong moment.

If that dog was a human, I'd stick him in the cells to remind him what happens to people who assault the sheriff. But he's a small, yappy dog, much loved in the town Ben assures me, and would probably poll better in the upcoming election than me.

I try not to think about the election. Ben and I have been together over a year now and I think my world is about to change again. Maybe once I'd have run uncontested, but not everyone is happy about having a gay sheriff, even worse a gay sheriff in a relationship with his much younger deputy. There are factions in the county who would love to see me ousted, particularly after the fallout with the business of Eric Kent. Sheriff Bob and I discovered the rot spread beyond my department. We cleaned house real well.

Ben tells me not to worry about it, Kent is gone now, but in the dark of the night I spend a lot of time staring up at the ceiling wondering what to do next. I've never been anything except a cop. I could become a deputy again and get back out in the field, but I'm not sure about taking a demotion. I like being the sheriff, even with all the politics. Ben mentioned me getting involved in actual politics. It's an idea but I'm not an activist, no matter how much 'gay sheriff' is mentioned. I just want to serve my county and live in my town.

And now Ben's my lover, everyone treats me like they do him. All smiles and no respect. I complain about it endlessly to Ben. He just shoves me against the wall and kisses me until I've forgotten what I was complaining about. He does that a lot.

I watch Ben and Will fuss and croon over Barky. The

demon dog is staying with us for a few days while Geraldine takes care of her sister. It wasn't my idea, no matter what Ben tells everyone, and that picture of me napping with Barky curled up in my arms—it's fake. I don't believe it happened. But it was up on Instagram before I woke up. Geraldine was thrilled and showed all her friends. And apparently my polling went up before I'd opened my eyes.

"JD?"

Ben's soft voice distracts me.

I flush. "Sorry, did you say something?"

"Are you taking Barky with you?"

I glower at his smirk. Barky coming to work with me was also not my idea. But we are both out at work all day and we can't leave him on his own. I want my house intact and Barky has sharp teeth.

"Yeah, I'll go home and change, then he can come with me."

To be fair, Barky is a good boy at the office. He curls up with Gloria and I don't see him until he needs to go potty. Why no one else will take him, I don't know, but Gloria loves on him, and he curls up in her lap as she takes the calls. She calls him her therapy dog. I point out they need training, but Gloria just croons over Barky and ignores me.

Ben bends down to pet the dog again, giving me a perfect view of his round ass in his uniform pants. He smirks at me when he straightens and catches me ogling his butt.

"I'll come with you," Ben says. "Aimee is going to be late today. She's visiting with Maggie. It's her first softball game today."

The little girl who was in a serious car accident on her seventh birthday has been adopted by the department as our mascot. It's been a long road to recovery for her but a year on, she's back playing sports and Aimee wanted to be at her game.

But Ben coming back with me is not a good idea. Ben and I usually part at CC's. His partner picks him up and I go home. When we go home together we get distracted. Usually against the wall. We end up being late.

But I can't think of a reason to protest and when Ben licks his lips and winks, why the heck would I want to? From the snort behind me, Ben is not subtle. He may as well write 'Let's fuck!' in skywriting. It's a good thing I've started our morning patrol of Collier's Creek early to allow for Barky's walk and quickies at home.

Sure enough, the second the door is closed, he's on me, undoing my shirt and dragging my pants down around my ankles.

"I need to leave in five minutes." My protest is pro forma at best.

Ben looks up from the floor. "It's a good thing I can bring you off in three."

He can. We timed it.

Barky gives a huff and heads for his favorite spot on the couch. He's learned that he's going to be ignored until we've climaxed. Who says you can't teach an old dog new tricks? I think that applies to him, and me.

My only rule for having Barky was he kept his paws on the floor. That lasted five seconds. But now I couldn't care less because Ben's mouth is on my cock and he's going for his maximum 'suck JD's balls through his dick' technique. I try to remember I'm old and should take things easy. Then my young lover does this and I think being old is a state of mind.

"Hold on," he warns me.

I card my fingers through his hair and hold on for dear life.

Three minutes and ten seconds later, he looks up, triumphant, a streak of cum across his lips.

"You're late and you missed a bit." I scoop it up and offer

it to him. He applies the same suction to my finger as he did to my dick.

"Ten seconds, seriously. That's allowed."

Then Ben strips me off and redresses me like I'm five with the fresh uniform which was waiting for me on the hall stand.

"You knew we were gonna do this."

He rolls his eyes at my accusation. "Of course I did. Five minutes. You're ready."

"What about you?" I don't like leaving my man hanging.

"You can make it up to me tonight."

"Clean your teeth," I suggest.

Ben jogs to the bathroom while I pack Barky's bag and pick up our lunches. Ben insists on making our lunches each day. God, I'm so lucky to have this man in my life. He gives me a minty kiss when he returns from the bathroom.

As we drive the short distance to the sheriff's office, he says, "I spoke to my momma yesterday."

I give him a quick glance. "Is she okay?"

The relationship between them has been strained since Ben moved in with me. She finds it difficult to have a son-in-law almost the same age as her and Ben used to help with chores and dealing with Sam. When he moved in he said he would help her but he wasn't on call 24/7 like he had been before. I try not to get between them, and be his rock when he needs me. Burl promised to talk to her too. I just have to be patient.

"Sam has agreed to go to rehab."

Again.

That's the word he missed out. His little brother is in and out of rehab. Personally, I think he'd do better going into the army. I'd seen it work for others. But I wasn't part of the family and Ben would hate it if I suggested it. He wants Sam where he can keep an eye on him.

What I had arranged was Will's partner and sports coach, Colton, to run summer camp for troubled teens like Sam. Colton had complained he didn't have enough time to woo his boyfriend, but I told him I had an in with said boyfriend. I should do. I spent enough in the coffee shop. Whatever, if it works on Sam, I owe Colton my firstborn.

Ben leans against my shoulder for a moment and I squeeze his thigh. Then we're at the office. I park next to the Dodge Gloria bought when she became a dispatcher. Ben taught her to park it expertly and peace reigns between us.

In the office, we go our separate ways. Barky to sit with Gloria, Ben to join the other deputies, and me to my office. For however long I could call the office mine.

I sit down at my desk and opened up my laptop, groaning at the number of emails that populate my inbox.

Then I saw one which caught my eye. It's from Ray Murphy.

"Word on the street is Collins is pulling out of the race. He doesn't want to be sheriff. He just didn't want you to be sheriff."

I knew that already, Martin Collins is a friend of the mayor and always disliked me. My sexuality was just another reason to hate me.

"He's the only one with a chance of beating you. Watch this space."

I take a breath, then another one. For the first time in months, maybe the light at the end of the tunnel isn't an oncoming train.

"Post more photos with the dog."

I grimace. Really?

"Not joking."

I want to share the news with Ben, even the crack about the dog, but I don't want anyone to overhear. I message him.

"I've got news."

The response is almost instantaneous. *"I can't wait to get home."*

I stare down at the message. I'm not sure what the series of emojis mean but I recognize the eggplant. I'm not that old. My cock hardens to press against my pants just at the thought.

I type a response.

"You. Me. The closet now!"

"Why, Sheriff. My boss wouldn't approve. It's against the rules."

"Fuck the rules," I mutter.

Except they're my rules. I implemented them so we could work together. No meeting in the closet. Dammit.

"I'm out with Aimee now. I'm sorry. But I promise you tonight, you can tell me your news, then rock my world."

"You've rocked my world since the day I met you."

I smile at my screen when he replies, tracing the words with my fingers.

"Right back atcha, my Sheriff of the Creek."

THE END

But not the end of the series. Did you notice how much time the sheriff spent gazing into the windows of Ellis Books?

Logan and Cooper have their enemies-to-lovers story in ALL THE WRONG PAGES, book #4 of Collier's Creek. Don't miss their story.

COLLIER'S CREEK SERIES

BECCA SEYMOUR
BEST KIND OF AWKWARD

ELLE KEATON
MANDATORY REPAIRS

SUE BROWN
SHERIFF OF THE CREEK

KATHERINE MCINTYRE
ALL THE WRONG PAGES

ALI RYECART
MEETING MR. ADORKABLE

NIC STARR
BLUE SKIES

ABOUT THE AUTHOR

Also by Sue Brown

You can find all of Sue's books over at <u>Amazon</u> and her website. Don't forget to sign up for her newsletter <u>here</u>.

About Sue Brown

Sue Brown is a Londoner with a dream to live on a small island. Coffee fuels her addiction to writing romance with hot guys loving each other, and her Adorkadog snores in harmony as she creates.

Come over and talk to Sue at:
Newsletter: http://bit.ly/SueBrownNews
Bookbub: <u>https://www.bookbub.com/profile/sue-brown</u>
TikTok: https://www.tiktok.com/@suebrownstories
Her website: http://www.suebrownstories.com/
Author group – Facebook: https://www.facebook.com/groups/suebrownstories/
Facebook: https://www.facebook.com/SueBrownsStories/
Email: <u>sue@suebrownstories.com</u>

Printed in Great Britain
by Amazon

33329912R00112